PON AVON • ROTHERHAM • BEXLEY • STANSTED • STOCKTON-ON-TE
TLE • NOTTINGHAM • DERBY • BARKING • MANCHESTER • LIVERPO
HAM • HEATHROW • PORTSMO HENLEY-ON-THAMES
AM • WATFORD • EGHAM • NOR OW • GRIMS
• CROYDON • CHEAM • LOUTH • READING

• WINCHESTER • SHEFFIELD • STRATFORD UPON AVON • ROTHERH
• IPSWICH • CROYDON • LICHFIELD • NEWCASTLE • NOTTINGH
A • GLASGOW • KING'S LYNN • BRISTOL • SUFFOLK • BIRMINGH
ES • RICHMOND • MANCHESTER • LEICESTER • LEEDS • MANCHEST
GRIMSBY • PORTSMOUTH • WHITSTABLE • NORWICH • LANCASTE
MSFORD • BRISTOL • YORK • MORECAMBE BAY • WATFORD • LOND
EXLEY • STANSTED • STOCKTON-ON-TEES • NEWCASTLE • EVESHAM
ARKING • MANCHESTER • LIVERPOOL • LONDON • SWANSEA • GLASG
HESTER • PORTSMOUTH • CARDIFF • HENLEY-ON-THAMES • RICHMON
• EGHAM • NORWICH • BOOTLE • HEATHROW • GRIMSBY • PORTSMOU
AM • LOUTH • BARKING • READING • CHELMSFORD • BRISTOL • YOR
ATFORD UPON AVON • ROTHERHAM • BEXLEY • STANSTED • STOCKT
• NEWCASTLE • NOTTINGHAM • DERBY • BARKING • MANCHESTE
SUFFOLK • BIRMINGHAM • HEATHROW • MANCHESTER • PORTSMOU
ER • LEEDS • LEWISHAM • WATFORD • EGHAM • NORWICH • BOO
ANCASTER • SNOWDONIA • CROYDON • CHEAM • LOUTH • BARKIN
Y • WATFORD • LONDON • WINCHESTER • SHEFFIELD • STRATFORD U
ASTLE • EVESHAM • IPSWICH • CROYDON • LICHFIELD • NEWCASTL

ONE MILLION TINY PLAYS ABOUT BRITAIN

BY THE SAME AUTHOR

Return to Akenfield

ONE MILLION TINY PLAYS ABOUT BRITAIN

Craig Taylor

BLOOMSBURY
LONDON · BERLIN · NEW YORK

First published in Great Britain 2009

Bloomsbury Publishing, London, Berlin and New York

36 Soho Square, London W1D 3QY

A CIP catalogue record for this book is available from the British Library

ISBN 978 0 7475 9791 9
10 9 8 7 6 5 4 3 2 1

Typeset by Hewer Text UK Ltd, Edinburgh
Printed by Clays Ltd, St Ives plc

The paper this book is printed on is certified by the © 1996 Forest Stewardship Council A.C. (FSC). It is ancient-forest friendly. The printer holds FSC chain of custody SGS-COC-2061

www.tinyplays.com

'When these miniature plays first started to appear in the *Guardian*, I thought that they were snippets of dialogue snatched from real life. Then I began to see that I'd been beguiled by Craig Taylor's craft – like the best playwrights, his characters have independent and spontaneous lives of their own contained within a carefully constructed dramatic architecture. Within his little worlds we see glimpses of the oddness, the quiet desperation, and the occasional tenderness of the lives of others. The plays are an original form: dramatic haikus. The fact that they're so short merely emphasises the skill with they've been put together. They're a wonderful keyhole through which you can peer at contemporary Britain'

Richard Eyre

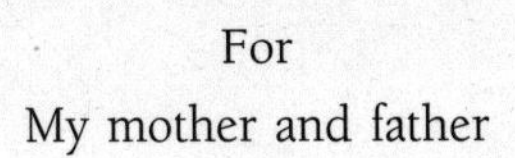

For

My mother and father

Introduction

A while back, my wife and I were in a hospital ward. On the adjacent bed, behind a screen, a doctor was interviewing a man who'd fronted up to A&E complaining of food poisoning caused by a dodgy curry. As the doctor quizzed him, his answers sketched an increasingly vivid picture. We overheard allusions to his divorce, the search for a place to live, the obstacles to attending checkups to stabilise his heart condition. His new joinery job, he conceded, 'takes getting used to after not working for so long.' In response to the doctor's probing about booze, he mused; 'Two or three. There's not much to do in the caravan, you understand. And then a couple more when I go to the pub.' By the end of the consultation – which might have been five minutes in total – our hero was informed that his vindaloo crisis was more likely to be withdrawal symptoms caused by abruptly reducing his alcohol intake from suicidal magnitude to a bog-standard unhealthy average. Behind the curtain, we felt we'd been privileged to witness a marvellously compressed little play. My wife leaned to me and whispered: 'If only Craig Taylor had been here.'

Craig Taylor wasn't there, but he's been in a great many other places where potent little dramas have played themselves out. Partly it's down to being a good listener: as a journalist, he specialises in interviews with so-called 'ordinary' people, and his first book *Return to Akenfield* was a documentary-portrait of rural England through the voices of its inhabitants. But the mini-plays collected here are not mere exercises in listening, no matter how convincingly they make us feel like eaves-droppers. At their best, they're cunningly shaped tragicomedies, in which the mundane truth of overheard conversation is fused with the higher truth of art. Sometimes, such as when the two bored garbage men conduct an elaborate *Waiting for Godot*-style argument about the deeper significance of rubbish, Taylor is happy to show his hand as a playwright. Sometimes, such as when the bloke at the car boot sale sums up his weekend in one laddish sentence, or when the young farmer passes judgement on drum 'n' bass in a withering one-liner, Taylor's role seems minimal, a human tape recorder switched on and off. Mostly, the pieces walk a fine line: so raw and authentic we want to believe they're unprocessed reportage, so tightly packed with meaning and so juicily satisfying we know they must be laced with fiction.

Modern Britain's messy demographics fascinate Taylor and he's exceptionally sensitive to the nuanced noises of cultural collision: the half-suppressed racism that spikes encounters between whites and blacks, the begrudging semi-tolerance of gays, the struggles of 'old-skool' humans to adjust to post-modern ways of doing things. Every reader will have different favourites, different moments when they feel like shouting 'Yes! That nails it exactly!' Giving further examples here is pointless, since each play can be read so quickly that a summary might be longer than the play itself – and would fail to get across what's special about Taylor's vignettes: their unfeasibly rich resonance. I will say only that the play in which an animal rights protester tries to wangle a petition signature from a youth who's impressed with the 'wicked' photo display is the sharpest piece of drama I'd read in a long time. These plays may be tiny in duration but their achievement makes the long, ponderously self-conscious works of many professional playwrights look small.

Michel Faber, November 2008

Play no. 1

(Two women stand in a queue at a bank in Richmond, Surrey)

Ellie I just can't picture it.
Eve Couldn't either.
Ellie Going to Paris with Izzy Mason?
Eve I wasn't going to say no. Not to a free trip.
Ellie She's just such a character, isn't she?
Eve She makes me die.
Ellie And swears. Can't believe her mouth sometimes.
Eve Should hear her husband.
Ellie That the one from the Christmas party?
Eve He was there when we got back. Picked us up from King's Cross, drove me home, swearing the whole way – Paki-this, Paki-that. Terrible. Was biting my tongue all the way to Battersea.
Ellie He the one with the scar?
Eve The what?
Ellie Is he the one with the big fat tummy and the hernia scar? At the Christmas party, he was lifting up his shirt and showing it off.
Eve Sounds right.
Ellie Awful.
Eve Oh, and she's always got trouble. We were talking about a show on the telly about men who use prostitutes, and Izzy started crying. Crying. She said it was too close to home – so horrible.

Ellie	But Paris, though . . .

Eve	We had a wonderful time.

Ellie	And that fast train . . .

Eve	So sleek. Izzy says, 'I'm going to take this train to Paris, throw myself in the Seine, never come back. You tell him that.'

Ellie	Such a character, she is, saying that.

Eve	She actually did try. On the Saturday.

(pause)

But you seen the watch?

Ellie	You showed me.

Eve	From Paris.

Ellie	Beautiful.

Eve	We both got one, Izzy and I. She deserves it.

Ellie	Oh, she does. She does.

Play no. 2

(A woman speaks to a young interviewee at a job interview in Durham)

Gail Perfectionist. Is that your answer?

Alice Yes. I'm just a bit too much of a perfectionist.

Gail And that is what you consider your greatest weakness as an employee?

Alice Yes. That's all.

Gail OK. I guess we can move on to the next question.

Alice Unless I should change that?

Gail No. Not if it's true.

Alice Because they say that's what you're supposed to say, isn't it?

Gail You're not supposed to say what you're told you're supposed to say. Just tell the truth.

Alice It's the truth, too.

(pause)

Gail Would you like to go back and answer the question again?

Alice Yes please.

Gail All right, we've heard about your strengths, Alice, now what do you consider to be a weakness?

Alice I got off with someone in the mailroom once.

Gail I don't know if that is what we consider an employment weakness.

Alice Because we weren't caught?

Gail No. I was looking more for something like 'I could improve my team skills'.

Alice Yes, he was my team leader.

Gail That's not really a weakness unless you're saying you'd repeat that behaviour in the future.

Alice Should I not put that one down?

Gail Well, it's not what we normally hear.

Alice Then can you just put it back to perfectionist?

Gail Fine.

Alice Because being a perfectionist is quite good as well as being bad.

Gail Now I'm looking at your reference.

Alice But you're not going to phone him though, are you?

Gail Your reference?

Alice Not after what I've just told you. Are you?

Gail Is that the name you put on the application?

Alice Yeah, and that's his home number and she'll probably answer and if you even say my name she'll go mental.

Gail The point of a reference, of course, is to phone them.

Alice She just thinks we're really close friends and all and she's always weird about it and the fact he once went to Liverpool to see me . . .

Gail I could call a mobile.

Alice . . . when he should have been at a conference in Bournemouth, even though nothing happened. That time.

Gail Then is there another reference you'd like us to use?

Alice No, because he said if I saw him once more he'd say whatever.

Gail Say whatever?

(pause)

Alice Could we go back to where I, like, talk about my visions for the job?

Play no. 3

(Two cars have collided at a roundabout in Watford. The drivers face each other)

Debbie . . . to have the courtesy to maybe get off the phone.

Tre I'm not on some phone, innit?

Debbie To just have some sort of courtesy. Because some people . . .

Tre And you're being all full of courtesy now are you?

Debbie Some people might get off their phone.

Tre Am I talking into it?

Debbie In a situation like this.

Tre It's a headset, yeah. It don't mean I'm on the phone. It's on my head.

Debbie And it's no wonder you did this, frankly, with that noise.

Tre Am I talking into my phone now, yeah?

Debbie It's no wonder you weren't concentrating with your bass making a godawful noise.

Tre You were the one stopped for no reason.

Debbie With your bass playing so loud. You can't even think. It's not as if I can't hear it.

Tre You talking about my music now, yeah?

Debbie Oh, do you want to call it music? Don't you think it was distracting you?

Tre Your radio's on.

Debbie Don't you think it draws your attention from the road?

Tre Your radio's on right now, yeah?

Debbie I am listening to Radio 4, all right? It's people speaking.

Tre It's radio. You're not concentrating.

Debbie It's English people speaking. I don't know . . .

Tre Oh, and I'm not listening to English people.

Debbie Listen, you little boy . . .

Tre Boy? Now you call us boy, yeah?

Debbie Young man, I will take photographs, young man, as evidence that you weren't concentrating, that your music was loud.

Tre And you stopped for no reason.

Debbie And you hit me. I will take photos on my phone right now. As evidence.

Tre Then do it.

Debbie I'm going to do it.

Tre Then take a photo on your phone.

Debbie I just did, all right? I won't be bullied. I won't be . . .

Tre You're texting.

Debbie What?

Tre You're not taking a photo. You're sending a text.

Debbie Oh.

Tre You got to use that button there. And hold your arm steady.

Play no. 4

(The HMV store on Oxford Street in London. A couple looks at CDs on the classical music floor)

Ellen Maybe we could get them Bach?

Dan Well, we could. I'm sure they probably don't need more Bach.

(pause)

Ellen Shostakovich?

Dan I think it's actually Shosta*ko*vich.

(pause)

Do you want to meet me downstairs? I'll only be a couple of minutes.

Play no. 5

(A father takes off his son's football boots in a park in Winchester)

Eric	Hey, Dad?
Dad	Yes, Eric.
Eric	I'm tired.
Dad	Nice to meet you, Tired. I'm Dad.
Eric	That's not even funny. Your jokes aren't even that funny, Dad.
	(pause)
	Hey, Dad?
Dad	Yes, Eric.
Eric	What was the score?
Dad	It was just a kickabout, really.
Eric	But what was the score?
Dad	Probably about 5–5.
Eric	But last goal wins, Dad.
Dad	Last goal wins in a way.
Eric	And they scored.
Dad	But your side was passing well.
Eric	That doesn't matter.
Dad	You passed it up to Sam like you were Paul Gascoigne.
Eric	Like I was who?
Dad	An old-time footballer. Who tied this knot on your shoe?
Eric	Sam's dad. He ties the tightest knots. Did you hear him yelling?
Dad	Yes, I heard Sam's dad.

Eric Yelling at Sam?

Dad I heard him.

Eric Me and Sam were practising our goal celebrations before the game. And Sam? Have you seen his new boots?

Dad I saw them.

Eric When he scores, he takes his shirt right off and starts waving it. But I'm going to do, like, a slide on my knees when I score. What was yours?

Dad I don't think we practised our celebrations.

Eric Why not?

Dad We mostly practised our passing. Football was a bit different back then.

Eric Sam says that if you're good when you're fifteen, you get paid £15m. And you get paid £16m if you're good when you're sixteen, and that's not even in the Premiership.

Dad He could buy his father a megaphone with that.

Eric But not if we keep losing.

Dad It was just a kickabout.

Eric I still don't like it.

Dad Give me your other boot.

Eric You never lose, Dad.

Dad Oh, I have, once or twice.

Eric I've never seen you lose.

Dad Give it a few years. You might.

(pause)

He tied these too tight. I'll cut them and buy you new laces.

Eric Or maybe some new boots? That's what I need. Dad?

Play no. 6

(An elderly woman stops a man at the gate to her house in Sheffield. He's holding an armful of flyers)

Agnes Excuse me? Excuse me? Sorry. Is this one of yours?

Atif Sorry?

Agnes Did you put this circular through the slot?

Atif I'm sorry, yes.

Agnes I heard a noise. I heard something coming through. I'm glad I caught you. I just wanted to ask you if this restaurant delivers. *(pause)*

This restaurant?

Atif Yes.

Agnes Delivers?

Atif Yes.

Agnes Does it make home deliveries?

Atif Yes.

Agnes To here? Do you understand what I'm saying? To here?

Atif Oh no.

Agnes So I'd have to go to the restaurant. Italian food, is it? And do you recommend the food?

Atif Yes.

Agnes Well, as I said, this just came through the door. I wasn't expecting it. I just wanted to know a little more. Where are you from? You're not from this country?

Atif Yes.

Agnes Where are you from? Your country?

Atif Yes. Pakistan.

Agnes Oh yes. My daughter toured Pakistan years ago. Before all the . . . There have been troubles, haven't there? I usually get to know the people who drop off the circulars. You must be new. My daughter owns the flat. She and her husband – he's a doctor – they live in Spain and I keep an eye on it. They're hoping to start a family. I just live downstairs, you see. I don't take up much space.

Atif Yes.

(pause)

Agnes Well. Just wanted to hear about your restaurant. I was. I was just reading in the newspaper about Charles and Camilla. Did you see last night's edition? I don't know about you but I was in favour of them marrying. It's good to have someone, isn't it, at that age? I tend to like her more. Even that hair. I don't know how you feel about it?

Atif Yes.

Agnes I loved my daughter's wedding because we had it in Spain because my son-in-law's practice, his medical practice, is over there. You must be married.

Atif Yes.

Agnes And your wife? She's back in Pakistan? You must be supporting her from afar, sending money. It's good to keep in touch. These phone cards should be making it easier to keep in touch. You'd think. Even if you're only as far away as Spain. You'd think people could just pick up the phone these days. Or rather you'd hope.

Atif Yes, but.

Agnes I'm sorry?

Atif But if you want delivery you call the number here.

Agnes If I want?

Atif Delivery.

(pause)

Agnes So you do deliver?

Atif Oh yes, yes.

(He laughs)

Agnes Oh.

(pause)

Agnes So you'll be coming back here? Do you come once a week?

Atif Yes. And takeaway.

Agnes No, but do you . . . You will be coming back here sometime? Because feel free to knock instead of putting circulars through the letterbox. I'm usually here.

Atif Yes.

(pause)

Agnes Do you have to go?

Atif Yes. I have more.

Agnes Thank you for stopping by. It was a very, very pleasant visit. I'll look this over. I'll sit down and take a look at it right now. Thank you, until I see you again.

Atif Yes.

Play no. 7

(A woman stands near the revolving door of an office block in Holborn, London, sandwich in hand. She speaks into a mobile phone)

Yeah.
Yeah.
Yeah.
Yeah.
Yeah. Oh yeah.
(pause)
(laughing) Yes.
Yeah.
Yeah.
Yeah.
Yeah.
Yeah.
Yeah.
Yeah.
(pause)
(affronted) Yes.
(confirming) Yes.
Yes, yes, yes.
Aw. Yeah.
Yes.
Yes.

(pause)

Yeah.

Oh yeah?

Yeah.

Yeah.

(pause)

(concerned) Yes.

(concerned) Yeah.

(concerned) Yeah.

(concerned) Yeah.

(sympathetic) Yeah.

(sympathetic) Yeah.

(pause)

(resolute) Yes.

Yes.

Yeah.

Yeah.

Yeah.

(with finality) Yes.

(pause)

(sceptical) Mmmm, yeah.

Yeah.

Yeah.

Yeah.

Yeah.

Yes.

Just, um, trying to eat my lunch.

I know it is.

No, I wasn't chewing into the phone.

Yes.

Yes.

Yeah.

Yeah.

We only get half an hour.

Yeah.

Yeah.

Yeah.

Yeah.

Yeah.

Yeah.

OK, Mum.

Yeah.

Yeah.

Yeah.

Yeah.

Yeah, yeah, yeah.

Bye.

Yeah.

Yeah.

Bye.

OK.

Yeah.

Yeah.

Yes.

Bye. Bye.

Play no. 8

(A man watches the proprietor of a veg stall in Stratford-upon-Avon)

Tom	I love the colour of your hands. You don't see hands that red these days.
Joe	Well, I see them quite a bit.
Tom	Real manual labour hands, aren't they? We've all got these soft, office-worker hands.
Joe	That's two quid for the tomatoes.
Tom	Exactly two quid? I'm good at this. I could do your job for you, couldn't I?
Joe	Probably not. *(pause)*
Tom	I love shopping local. I used to have an organic vegetable box delivered, but I had to stop. All that kale.
Joe	I like kale.
Tom	I love kale. Couldn't eat it for every meal, though.
Joe	I could.
Tom	Yes, I guess I could have tried. Are your potatoes local?
Joe	Local enough. They're not from bloody Spain.
Tom	I had some lovely produce in Spain.
Joe	I'm not a big fan of Spanish fruit.
Tom	Of course. Your potatoes look nice. Bit dirty, though.
Joe	They come from the dirt.
Tom	Sure. But now they come from you.

Joe You don't have to eat the dirt, mate.

Tom But, you see, the dirt adds to the weight. It all adds up.

Joe Does it now?

Tom Maybe you could give me a dirt discount?

Joe Would you like a dirt discount?

(pause)

Tom It's terrible that everything's individually wrapped in the supermarkets now. Every green pepper.

Joe It's disgusting is what it is.

Tom But then, on the other hand, their vegetables are very clean.

Joe You want me to rub these potatoes clean for you? Would you like that? With my hands?

Tom Um.

(pause)

No. I'll pick some up later. Busy day.

Play no. 9

(A farmer sits on a tractor in a field in Kent speaking into his mobile phone)

. . . and he thinks he's gone in a new direction when it's just the same shit.
(pause)
Drum and bass is dead to me, mate. It's dead to me.

Play no. 10

(Two men stand at a bar in the City. The NatWest building is visible out of one of the windows. They've put their briefcases at their feet)

Michael	Don't get me wrong. Most of Personnel is fine. Only a few have their airs and graces. For this project it would be a question of finding someone who knows when to stop talking as much as she knows when to start.
Harry	Or he knows when to start.
Michael	I beg your pardon?
Harry	You said she. But in my experience I've had plenty of problems with the men in Personnel.
Michael	Of course, of course. Yes, you're absolutely right. *(pause)* Though the men don't seem to be quite as diffident, do they?
Harry	Well, there's that.
Michael	You've seen it too?
Harry	To a certain extent.
Michael	You've noticed? I'm glad someone else has. I was beginning to feel I was on my own with that observation. I don't know the right word for it.
Harry	No, an adjective doesn't immediately come to mind.
Michael	Is 'uppity' too strong?
Harry	Hard to say, isn't it? *(pause)*

Michael	You see, the other problem is our emails just aren't being picked up by members. Half of them don't check their team accounts for messages concerning meeting times.

Harry	Yes, I know.

Michael	Even I only check mine when I absolutely have to. It gets filled with such unsolicited nonsense. People don't want to open up their accounts to deal with an avalanche of messages they didn't even ask for.

Harry	It's a huge problem these days.

Michael	'Do you need help with your creditors?' That sort of thing.

Harry	Yes.

Michael	'How about some cheap plane tickets to Jamaica?'

Harry	I believe I received that one too.

Michael	But you know what the worst is?

Harry	No, I don't.

Michael	The worst is the pornography. It just comes from out of nowhere.

Harry	Yes, I agree. Somehow they get your name from a list or what have you . . .

Michael	'Hot Lesbians' and such.

Harry	Their tactic is to flood your mailbox with more and more messages even if you write back asking them not to. It's awful. *(pause)*

Michael	You ever take a peek at it?

Harry	No, I can't say that I have.

Michael	No, me neither. I find that sort of thing has no effect on me. Hot, licking lesbians. Seems just ridiculous.
(pause)
There was even one for Scottish lesbians. Scottish lesbians. And they were supposedly tied to each other somehow, if

you can believe that. Some sort of contraption of knots apparently.

(pause)

Right. Well, what do you say? Shall we have another?

Harry I shouldn't really stay. Train's at quarter past.

Michael Even a half?

Harry Perhaps just a half.

Michael Good man. Good man.

Play no. 11

(A man, his wife and his wife's elderly mother are in a restaurant in Rotherham. The wife wears maternity clothing. A waitress is bringing their order)

Waitress	Here we are. Prime steak?
Eric	Here.
Waitress	Burger?
Eric	That's for her.
Waitress	Steak and kidney?
Eric	That's for her.
Pam	Looks fine, though, doesn't it?
Eric	Look what they've done with the chips. Mum? What do you think?
Jean	I'm not very hungry.
Eric	Mum, those are called fat chips. That's what you ordered. Fat chips, yeah? They'll fill you up.
Waitress	And how about any mustard? Any missing gravy?
Eric	No.
Waitress	Everyone's got everything they like?
Eric	Oh yeah.
Waitress	Sauces?
Eric	We're fine.
Waitress	Brown sauce?
Eric	No, we're fine.

Waitress Salad cream?

Eric We're just fine.

Waitress Right. Then I'd like you all to just thoroughly enjoy your meal.

(She leaves)

Eric Funny thing to say.

Pam What's that?

Eric *Thoroughly* enjoy your meal.

Pam Well she's just, you know . . . It's training nowadays. They're trained.

(pause)

Eric Do you want another half-pint then, Mum?

Pam Mum, Eric's asking if you'd like another half.

Jean Oh, no.

Eric *(to the waitress)* Excuse me. One more half-pint, would you, luv?

Jean Oh, no.

Eric Mum says no but I think she means yes, don't you, Mum? Do you know what you're having for pudding Mum?

Pam Eric, we've just started.

Eric But Mum's got a sweet tooth, hasn't she?

Jean I don't think I should have another half-pint of beer.

Eric I'm having a bit of cake for pudding. Can't wait for the cake, can we Mum? What are you having then, sweetheart?

Pam I don't know.

Eric Then pick. Come on. What're you having?

Pam I don't know what it's called. The one I always . . . the one with the fruit and the raspberry sauce and whatnot.

Eric The Horn of Plenty.

Pam If that's what it's called.

Eric	You already got one horn of plenty eight months ago, didn't you?
Pam	Don't talk like that in front of Mum.
Eric	Mum doesn't mind, does she Mum?
Jean	I don't mind.
Eric	Mum's got a bit of a sense of humour, don't you Mum?
Jean	She shouldn't be pregnant again so soon after the first baby.
Eric	What was that Mum?
	(pause)
	What was that?
	(pause)
Jean	I can't eat these. I ordered chips.
Pam	Those are chips, Mum.
Jean	They're not chips.
Pam	They're the ones called fat chips. They're just bigger but they're chips.
Jean	I can't eat these.

Play no. 12

(A Waitrose in north London. A man puts a bottle of red wine into his shopping basket. He speaks into his mobile)

I've just landed. I'm standing at the baggage carousel right now.

. . .

I don't know, sweetheart. I honestly can't say. You know how long it takes, especially at bloody Heathrow. I could be standing here for hours before any of the suitcases even appear. And I have no idea what the traffic is like getting into town.

. . .

Of course. Of course I do. I've been waiting months for it too.
(He picks up a bottle of white, considers it, puts it into his basket, quietly)
I will be there as soon as I possibly can. All right. I think the first suitcase is coming now. No, it's stopped.

. . .

I'm excited too. I can almost taste your kiss.

. . .

OK. Bye. Bye.

Play no. 13

(Two men stand at the urinals in a pub in Bexley)

Terry Fantastic strike, yeah?

Ritchie His finishes is superhuman.

Terry He's incredible, is what he is – I don't care what anyone says.

Ritchie And that was a work of art.

Terry More than any painting in some art gallery.

Ritchie More than some sculpture in a museum that's not even moving.

Terry You see his leg when he hit the ball?

Ritchie Brutal. He's like an animal.

Terry The muscles of his legs in slow motion – they were gigantic.

Ritchie Like a horse.

Terry Like some enormous, mythical . . . horse, yeah. I could see his muscles literally rippling as the ball came off his boot.

Ritchie Do you know what part of Africa he's from?

Terry He's from Africa.

Ritchie Yeah, but which country?

Terry One of those little ones, isn't it?

Ritchie One of those with a civil war?

Terry That's right, because he's always having charity kickabouts with kids with missing legs and such.

Ritchie Must be hard to play against kids on crutches.

Terry He's not going full out, though, doing slide tackles and trying to win.

Ritchie But those kids might hit him with a crutch or something.

Terry Not if he's paying their families.

Ritchie Still, you wouldn't want to risk playing against kids like that.

Terry I know, not when you've got worry about Champions' League next week.

Ritchie I can't stop thinking about that strike.

Terry Brilliant stuff. Brilliant. It was so good I can't even wee right now, you know what I mean?

Ritchie Me neither.

(pause)

What do you do when you can't wee?

Terry Just stand here for a bit.

Ritchie Yeah, me too. I try to clear my mind.

(pause)

I've got to stop thinking about that strike.

Terry I know. What a footballer, mate. What a footballer.

Play no. 14

(Two police officers have stopped a young man on his bicycle in Kennington, south London)

Police 1	We'd probably let you go if you hadn't lied.
Man	I never lied.
Police 2	What colour was it?
Man	Fine, then. Red, then.
Police 1	Why did you say it was amber?
Man	Because it was amber.
Police 2	Then how did we both see you cycle through a red light?
Man	You think I know that? Maybe you don't see colour so well. Maybe I look white to you.
Police 2	You don't look white to us. *(pause)*
Police 1	Nice bicycle.
Man	Yeah, it is.
Police 1	A little small for you.
Police 2	You didn't want to buy a proper sized one?
Police 1	When you went to the shop?
Police 2	When did you buy that bicycle, Derek?
Man	I never bought it.
Police 2	Really? You never bought it?
Police 1	That's surprising.

Man	Because it's my brother's.
Police 2	He likes pink bikes, does he, Derek? Small bikes, Derek?
Man	Why you calling me that? It's not my name.
Police 2	What's your name?
Man	It's . . . you know.
Police 1	No, we don't know.
Man	It's Chilly.
Police 2	That's not what it says on your driving licence.
Police 1	Why does it say Derek?
Police 2	What's Chilly? Is that your hip hop name?
Man	It's my name.
Police 1	Your gangsta name?
Man	It's my name.
Police 1	Do you know what my hip hop name would be? Bizzy.
Police 2	Why's that?
Police 1	Because I get busy. I'm generally a busy person.
Police 2	See, we both like hip hop.
Police 1	Respect.
	(pause)
Police 2	So is it Chilly, Derek?
Police 1	Put on a jumper.
Police 2	If you're Chilly.
	(pause)
Man	Does that mean I can go?
Police 1	You listen to 50 Cent, Derek?
Man	No.
Police 1	What are you listening to? Those are some pretty nice headphones.

Police 2	They must be your brother's too?
Man	They're mine.
Police 2	Like the bike.
Police 1	Now, when I ask you what colour that light was what are you going to say? Chilly?
Man	Amber. Whatever.
	(pause)
	Red.

Play no. 15

(A couple sits drinking coffee at Stansted airport)

Amy	Oh.
Joe	But I just sat there. Honestly, I didn't do anything. I was just keeping him company.
Amy	Even though you said no cafés, no drugs on this trip.
Joe	I didn't want drugs. He needs weed. Mikey needs it like I need air.
Amy	You both said, 'We're going for the Rembrandts.' Not drugs.
Joe	Not hard drugs. It wasn't crack. But you know Amsterdam. You get there and it's just so . . . Amsterdammish.
Amy	How much did you have?
Joe	Nothing – I was just with him.
Amy	Except a toke.
Joe	To keep him company – you know how lonely he looks when he has a spliff. He looks like a beagle.
Amy	Then I suppose you ate a brownie.
Joe	Yeah, but they don't even label what's in them in those cafés.
Amy	How was the Rijksmuseum?
Joe	Yeah. Good. Big. *(pause)*
Amy	Did you see the Rembrandt painting of the steam engine going into the tunnel?
Joe	Of course. Great use of light. And dark, which he's known for. *(pause)*

Amy And how was the hotel?

Joe Very Dutch.

Amy Or was it a B&B you stayed at? Because you left a number for a B&B.

Joe It had a hotel feel. Very officious.

Amy I guess that's why the woman who runs it said you hadn't shown up when I called this morning.

Joe Well, we didn't sleep there, if that's what you meant by 'stayed'.

Amy If I asked Mikey, would he say you passed out on the same park bench as last time?

Joe No. I mean, he passed out. I didn't. I just didn't feel like sleeping.

Amy For Amsterdammish reasons?

Joe Sure.

(pause)

And also because of the handcuffs.

Amy I see.

Joe They use these plastic ones now.

Amy Oh.

Play no. 16

(A man stands at a car boot sale in Stockton-on-Tees)

Well, answer your own question. I did 1,800 miles in the caravan and drank three gallons of cider. So I'll ask you whether or not it was a good weekend.

Play no. 17

(Two women lean against each other at the Quayside in Newcastle. One is dressed as Wonder Woman, the other as Supergirl)

Julie My shoes.

Debbie I know, Julie.

Julie What happened to my shoes, then? You know what they cost me?

Debbie The taxi ran over them when you was fighting.

Julie I'll hit her again till she pays for them. I will.

Debbie The taxi ran over hers, too.

Julie Did you hear what she said to me in the club?

Debbie I couldn't hear a thing in there.

Julie Me neither – but she said something, she did, the slag.

Debbie You tore out some of her hair.

Julie What's she doing dressed as Wonder Woman, anyway?

Debbie She's on a hen night, is all.

Julie But why's she got to be Wonder Woman? There's not two of 'em.

Debbie Maybe she went to another fancy-dress shop.

Julie Do you think hers is better?

Debbie It's tighter, isn't it?

Julie I said I wanted the tightest.

Debbie Look how it holds her tits up.

Julie My tits don't need to be held up.

Debbie Hers doesn't have that dark patch on the bottom like yours.

Julie Don't tell Jason I hit a Wonder Woman. Even though she's a slag.

Debbie He can't call off the wedding just 'cos you've done more fighting.

Julie It's too late to call it off.

Debbie And you're not getting arrested this time, are you?

Julie He'd probably think she's a better Wonder Woman, anyway.

Debbie You know that's not true.

Julie He'd look at her and think, 'Why are my Wonder Woman's tits so low?' I can't help it.

Debbie Julie?

Julie What?

Debbie Julie, look at me. Don't think that. He loves you. And wait until the baby gets here.

Julie Did I pull out more hair than her?

Debbie Much more.

Julie Was it a handful?

Debbie It was plenty.

Julie He'd be proud of that, wouldn't he? Of his Wonder Woman?

Debbie Of course.

Julie I think I'm actually going to be sick. A bit.

Play no. 18

(A funeral director sits close to a crying woman at a funeral home in Evesham, Worcestershire)

James And, of course, I'm here for you.

Jane You'll need some details.

James That's right – about his life, his interests, to get a picture of what a great fellow he was.

Jane He was a football fan, obviously.

James Of course. What team?

Jane David Beckham.

James That's more an individual.

Jane He loved him. Looked up to him.

James So, for 'team' we could put down Manchester United, perhaps? I support Man U, so I know exactly how it feels to want to be buried in red.

Jane He didn't mention Man U.

James He wasn't saying much near the end, though.

Jane He was just a fan of Beckham.

James But Beckham's best years were at Manchester United. Ask anyone. I have a Man U banner we can drape over the coffin. And that's free.

Jane I don't want a flag draped over.

James Then we'll hang it behind.

Jane He had his Beckham shirt – I'd like him to be wearing that.

James A red one, I imagine.

Jane No, white – from Madrid. He wore it in hospital just days before. Before . . .

James Take a moment. That's right.

Jane It just hung off his body . . .

James These are hard times. Hard decisions you must face. But would he really want to be buried in the kit of a Spanish team?

Jane It was just a shirt. His last shirt.

James Did he even speak Spanish?

Jane Of course not.

James Right. Perhaps I can find a Manchester United shirt for him.

Jane I held him in that shirt. I want it.

James Then you might as well bury him in an LA Galaxy shirt.

Jane I'm sorry?

(pause)

James I'm just saying we're here for you. I said he's probably looking down on us from some star in the galaxy. That's right. Our banner will look lovely. It's what he'd have wanted.

Play no. 19

(A couple sits in a restaurant in west London)

Richard I've got another tissue.

Sara No thank you.

Richard If you need it.

(He puts it down next to her knife)

Sara I don't need it.

(She wipes her nose on the back of her hand)

(She dabs at her eyes with her finger)

So.

Richard So. That's that, then.

Sara I think I'm going to drink some more wine.

(He fills her glass)

Richard Simon recommended this place.

Sara It seems like a Simon type of place.

Richard He says hello.

Sara Does he?

Richard He hopes this won't mean you'll disappear from his and Patricia's life.

Sara Really? I'm sure that's what he said. This must be the greatest day of his year. He can finally have you to himself. He won't have to put up with my droning interruptions at dinner parties ever again.

Richard He didn't say droning.

Sara — My 'interruptions' at dinner parties.

Richard — It was a joke and he didn't mean it. You know that.

(pause)

Richard — He recommended the mussels.

Sara — I find they tend to drone.

(pause)

Richard — Well, I would just like to say that I would like to arrange a time to pick up my clothes and belongings.

Sara — Well, I would just like to say that I can have them sent to you.

Richard — I don't want to put you through that.

Sara — I can pack objects, Richard. All your clothes are out of the wardrobe anyway.

Richard — I don't want you to.

Sara — Am I going to find something?

Richard — You're not going to find anything.

Sara — Did you burn your receipts? Did you tear up all her letters?

Richard — There are no letters.

Sara — No, sorry, of course. I must be droning on.

Richard — Simon has offered me a room in his house.

Sara — His own room?

Richard — No.

Sara — Is he divorcing Patricia to be with you? That would be perfect, wouldn't it? You wouldn't have to hurry down the street to the Nag's Head to spend all Saturday talking about how you wished you never had to come back home. You could just stay in bed with each other, couldn't you?

Richard — There's no need to be angry with him.

Sara	Why are you living at his house, Richard? A family with an infant doesn't need a lodger. Why don't you just move back to Shepherd's Bush like any ordinary person would?
Richard	Because I'm going to be a father.
	(pause)
Sara	Oh.
	(She pours herself more wine)
	And. And I suppose this woman is going to move into Simon and Patricia's house?
Richard	No. She won't exactly have to move in.
Sara	You're having a child with Patricia?
Richard	Don't be ridiculous.
Sara	Then.
	(pause)
	The girl.
Richard	She is not 'the girl'.
Sara	That girl. You're just sitting here telling me this. Good God. She can't even speak. She can't even speak whatever it is. Ukrainian, or whatever it is. She looks like your niece, is what she looks like. She's fifteen.
Richard	She's not fifteen.
Sara	She speaks Ukrainian in that voice. She dropped Patricia's serving dish and yelled at the baby in whatever language. She's fifteen years old and she's hired and . . .
	(pause)
	You won't have children. You said.
Richard	I never said. This wasn't planned.
Sara	We planned for later.
Richard	We did not.
Sara	We did.

Richard	We never planned.
	(pause)
Sara	I was there. I was probably in the next room, wasn't I?
Richard	You're not going to do this here.
Sara	At their solstice party? Is that when? Was I outside the closet?
Richard	No.
Sara	You're going to say you brought her back to our flat.
Richard	Do you really want to know where? In Worcestershire and it was at my parent's house and I drove her there. She had never seen the country. It was not in a closet.
Sara	I was sitting at home.
Richard	No, you were at another one of your weddings somewhere.
	(pause)
Sara	Well. I guess it's hard to get out and see the country when you're working for a family. Did she tell you how beautiful it was in Ukrainian?
Richard	I don't expect you to understand.
Sara	It must be quite beautiful seeing it through someone else's eyes.
Richard	When was the last time you asked me about the name of a tree? Or what kind of leaves were on the ground? When was the last time you noticed anything that wasn't in a Habitat catalogue?
Sara	Were there leaves on the ground then, Richard?
	(pause)
	Then why are you telling me in March?
Richard	There were considerations.
Sara	You touched me. You slept in our bed.
Richard	I couldn't tell you right away, if you have to know.

Sara Why?

Richard Fine. We had to find out if the baby was Simon's or if it was mine.

(pause)

Sara I see.

Play no. 20

(A woman stands at a newsagent's stall)

Woman	*(holding up a copy of* Cosmopolitan*)* Isn't there one more recent than this?
Newsagent	That's this month's. New one not for . . . two weeks.
Woman	Fine. And a Coke please. *(pause)* No, sorry. Diet Coke.

Play no. 21

(A woman cuts a man's hair in a salon in Hammersmith)

Lucja It takes twenty-four hours to get here from my home.

Pat I can't sit on a coach for even an hour.

Lucja English are so weak.

Pat No, it's my bad back.

Lucja Try sitting twenty-four hours from east of Poland. At the end, my legs were concrete.

Pat That would do terrible things to my old back.

Lucja My head was stone. My hands were shaking. They wouldn't stop shaking. See? How short do you want the sides?

Pat Um. Not too short.

Lucja I will just keep cutting.

Pat Are you going to use those scissors?

Lucja They look bad. They still work.

Pat I don't think they're meant for hair.

Lucja They will cut through. It's just hair.

Pat Where's the woman who cut my hair last time?

Lucja She is Bulgarian.

Pat What does that mean?

Lucja She is gone. You know, when I get here there was nothing. England gives you nothing. Never a good job.

Pat What kind of salon did you work at in Poland?

Lucja I never worked in salon.

Pat Oh. I see.

Lucja Why would anyone ever work in salon? So stupid.

Pat You do now.

Lucja I hate all this touching hair. I used to work in . . . what's the word? I kill animals by hitting them on head.

(pause)

Pat I think it's an abattoir.

Lucja For killing. I'm not afraid of blood.

Pat Maybe not too short on the sides.

Lucja But you must be smart when killing. I check for dirty things in meat.

Pat Parasites.

Lucja Do you know how many could fit on this comb?

Pat I think I'll keep that back part quite long. Just as it is, really.

Play no. 22

(A young couple walk past the rides at a steam fair in York)

Tim It's not the manic kind, though. Just the regular kind.

Lou And it's under control?

Tim Yeah.

Lou You didn't want to mention it sooner?

Tim It's not a great first-date topic.

Lou Or second, apparently.

Tim I don't like telling every single person I meet.

Lou And should you be drinking?

Tim Not officially. But I want it to be a memorable sort of night. Don't you?

Lou Sure. Yes. So, what are you like when you're not taking them?

Tim Oh, totally the same. Sort of the same. A little down sometimes.

Lou Nothing too bad?

Tim God, no. I sort of stayed in bed in June. But . . .

(pause)

Do you want to go on one of the rides?

Lou Sure. Can you go on them?

Tim Yeah. I used to be so scared of that one.

Lou Being spun around and all?

Tim No, I mean, I used to be really scared. Really anxious.

Lou How do you feel about them now?

Tim Fine. I don't feel much about them, to be honest.

Lou	Is that because of the medication?

Tim	Not exactly.

(pause)

Did you like your flowers? I wasn't sure if you were a wild flower kind of girl.

Lou	I loved them. Thank you.

Tim	Great. I'm good at doing things like that. Nice things.

Lou	Are you on a really high dosage?

Tim	No. It's hardly anything.

Lou	But you have been on them for a while?

Tim	You know what, I don't think I should have mentioned it.

Lou	You weren't going to say anything?

Tim	No, of course I was. Just don't look scared.

Lou	Should I be scared?

Tim	No. They just make things a little better. Me a little better.

Lou	Except you said you were just the same.

REDUCE
SPEED
NOW
WORKS
ENTRANCE
AHEAD
150YDS

Play no. 23

(A government official speaks to a child
at an asylum seekers' screening unit in Croydon)

. . . An X is not a tick.
Could you please tell them that?
Could you tell them that now?
Could you translate that for your parents?
This is very, very important.
An X – can you hear what I'm saying? An X is not a tick.

Play no. 24

(Two elderly women finish their tea at a café in Lichfield. One holds the bill)

Anna Oh, you. Now don't be so utterly ridiculous.

Eva I insist. I insist, my dear.

Anna Absolutely not and I won't hear another word from silly old you.

Eva Well, I won't hand it over.

Anna You give it to me right now.

Eva I won't. I won't, and that's the end of it.

Anna I can't have you paying for this, can I?

Eva You paid for the last tea.

Anna And that was nearly a year ago, silly.

Eva Exactly. Just put that wallet away now, you troublemaker.

Anna That's enough. Give it to me.

Eva I'm going to pay and that's that.

Anna Then I'm putting some money in your purse.

Eva You're going nowhere near my purse.

Anna I need to say thank you.

Eva Then a simple thank you's enough.

Anna You know how I feel about this, dear.

Eva Well, fair is fair.

Anna I don't believe it is fair, if you don't mind.

Eva Then you can take me out for a nice meal next time, can't you?

Anna	This is my treat.
Eva	It is completely my treat and I want to pay. The end.
Anna	No.
	(pause)
Eva	Now sit down. I'm just going to put it on my credit card and we'll go on with our lovely afternoon.
Anna	Tell me how much it is.
Eva	And we'll see the dahlias out in Biddulph.
Anna	I'll sit right here then. I'll just sit.
Eva	Well, you're being silly.
Anna	You're being silly.
Eva	I don't want your money. A simple thank you is fine.
Anna	I'd like to give you some money.
Eva	Just say thank you now. Just say it.

Play no. 25

(An employee speaks to a member of the IT helpdesk at a company in Belfast)

Dean Well, I certainly won't do it again.

Ian Just answer yes or no. Do you understand the consequences?

Dean I have a hard time believing the consequences could be that severe.

Ian Yes or no?

Dean Fine. Yes.

Ian Because I think I told you about the last person to plug in their personal laptop to our system.

Dean You said it caused chaos.

Ian OK, chaos? It's more like what's called superchaos.

Dean I don't believe that's a word.

Ian It's an IT term, a professional IT term. Let's just say you could have toppled the entire infrastructure of the company by plugging in.

Dean I very much doubt that.

Ian Oh, sorry, so now you're the IT expert?

Dean No.

Ian I actually didn't know I was speaking to another IT expert who had trained as much as me and got qualifications.

Dean I'm just saying my computer is safe.

Ian And that's because you have a complete and ongoing list of every virus in the world?

Dean I do have virus software.

Ian So do most of the cyberterrorists creating the new viruses, or what's known as computer virii.

Dean We're a stationery company. I don't think cyberterrorists are targeting us.

Ian And I guess you don't play Warcraft.

Dean No, no, I don't play video games.

Ian Attacks come from all sides. It's a hard but necessary lesson.

Dean We're talking about a single laptop here.

Ian You don't know what's been hidden inside. You've heard of the Trojan pony?

Dean No, I haven't.

Ian It's a Roman myth about a large pony stuffed with explosives. Everyone thinks it's innocent until it goes off. It kills and maims hundreds.

Dean I think you might actually be referring to the Trojan horse. From *The Iliad*?

(pause)

Ian No, I'm not.

Dean Fine, then.

Ian The Trojan pony is actually an IT term, a professional IT term. OK? Have I been clear? Have I made myself perfectly clear in this situation?

Play no. 26

(Two older women work in the cloakroom of a theatre in Nottingham)

Joyce	They don't even taste like mints.
Jean	Wait till you get to the middle.
Joyce	Is it soft in the middle, then?
Jean	Delicious, really.
Joyce	And minty?
Jean	More minty than last night's.
Joyce	Which coat did they come from?
Jean	That red one.
Joyce	Lovely pattern on it.
Jean	You should try it on.
Joyce	I might after the interval.
Jean	It's good someone's still wearing coats like that. *(pause)* Shall we have another mint?
Joyce	It passes the time, doesn't it?
Jean	You know, I swear I won't go into some of these newer coats.
Joyce	You don't know what you'll find.
Jean	The pockets are full of rubbish.
Joyce	And Skittles.
Jean	I would never eat a Skittle.
Joyce	You can tell a lot from someone's pockets.

Jean I once took Diana Rigg's coat – in her pocket was a packet of Polos.

Joyce That's an elegant mint.

Jean I ate three.

Joyce For an elegant woman I would say.

Jean I don't think she even noticed.

Joyce That's the most famous coat we've had here.

Jean Except for the Lloyd Webber.

Joyce There was never a Lloyd Webber.

Jean You were off that night.

Joyce And you never mentioned it before?

Jean You never asked.

Joyce That would've passed the time.

Jean I was almost scared to go in his pockets. It sat there all first half. I finally put my hand in. The pockets were deep and lined with strange fur. I could sense something at the bottom.

Joyce Out with it.

Jean It was a half-eaten HobNob.

Joyce Surely he'd finish it at least.

Jean I think he's gone downhill. I couldn't even watch *Cats* after that.

Joyce I won't believe it.

Jean And him being a life peer and everything. He could have finished it. Fancy another mint?

Joyce I've not finished mine yet.

Jean I've just finished mine. Mind you, I nibbled the last bit, didn't I?

Play no. 27

(A young man approaches the counter of a used record shop in Derby)

Bill	Cash or trade?
Tim	Yeah, just trade.
Bill	Even this *Blonde On Blonde*?
Tim	God, yeah. Christmas present. I only played it once.
Bill	They didn't know you already owned it.
Tim	I don't.
Bill	On vinyl, I mean.
Tim	No, mate, it's not my thing.
Bill	Oh yeah? I guess it's only the most essential album of all time in a few circles these days.
Tim	Not a big fan of him.
Bill	'Him'? Sort of like saying you're not a fan of breathing.
Tim	I never heard anything by Breathing.
Bill	My wife would actually call the police if I traded in any Dylan. It's the first sign of madness, especially since *B On B* was playing in the room when my first daughter was born.
Tim	Yeah, it's just a bit old.
Bill	Oh yeah? You'll be trading in the Sistine Chapel next.
Tim	Mate, I've never heard their stuff either. I'm sort of into the new.

Play no. 28

(Two mothers stand near a Santa's grotto in Barking)

Sue	It's absolutely ingenious. It fits in his little hand.
Jill	And is it silent?
Sue	Oh yeah. He just presses the button and this alarm goes off where I can hear it.
Jill	In your handbag?
Sue	Of course. I'll be watching him the whole time.
Jill	I think I should buy one.
Sue	They're not too pricey. We did a practice run before we came, just to tell him what Santa might try.
Jill	I won't let my daughter even sit near Santa.
Sue	It's not just the touching. I read there are paedo Santas who groom children for years.
Jill	With just words?
Sue	Year after year.
Jill	Where did you read that?
Sue	The newspaper.
Jill	Which paper?
Sue	All of them, really.
Jill	I just get so worried. I didn't even want to bring her.
Sue	But it is Christmas, isn't it?
Jill	I didn't want to bring her.
Sue	With an alarm she'll be fine.

Jill We used to be able to trust Santa.

Sue It's everywhere you look. He's got a teacher who gives all the pupils Valentine cards.

Jill Unbelievable.

Sue This is a grown man giving out Valentines to children. I kept my son's card in case it's needed as evidence.

Jill It's frightening.

Sue Because you read about paedo teachers, don't you?

Jill I guess I do.

Sue And, worse than that, you read about these paedo elves.

Jill I haven't seen that.

Sue In the newspaper.

Jill Which one?

Sue It's been everywhere. The parents are too busy worrying about Santa.

Jill And not thinking about the elves.

Sue It's been all over the news.

Jill Just awful.

Play no. 29

(Two young people stand outside a pub in Clapham. Their pints of Stella Artois are almost finished. The night is clear)

Jo It's so weird how your tolerance just goes down so much. Isn't that weird?

John You haven't had anything to drink for ten days?

Jo Twelve days.

John Twelve whole days.

Jo I've been a good girl.

John You have.

Jo But it's a Friday, you know?

John You can't hold back on Friday night.

Jo I said to myself: tonight, John is in town . . .

John That's right.

Jo He's taken a train all the way to see me.

John And the rest of the gang, yeah.

Jo I'm going to let myself go.

John Well, we've had a few.

Jo And I'm going to tell him how I feel.

John You're feeling good, aren't you? We're feeling good. Nice spring night.

Jo John.

John What's the matter? Here. Come over here.

Jo John. How long have we been friends?

John I don't know. Nearly six months, I guess.

Jo No, John. It's been two years.

John I met you two years ago.

Jo And we were friends.

John Well, not friends right away. Acquaintances. At least at the beginning. I mean, I knew who you were.

Jo John.

John Do you want to sit down?

Jo I'm fine. John.

John Yes, Jo?

Jo John. We have been friends for three years. And I have loved you . . .

(pause)

Whoops.

(pause)

I wasn't supposed to get to that part until a few minutes later.

(pause)

Do you hate me now that I've said that?

John Now that you've said what?

Jo You know. What I just said.

John I love you too, Jo. I think you're great. I think you're brilliant.

Jo John.

John Yes?

Jo John. I don't want to sleep with you.

John Jo, I'm sort of seeing someone up in Manchester. I have a girlfriend.

Jo Not that I haven't thought, oh, you know, something like 'I wouldn't mind if he took my bra off.'

John I'm kind of unavailable, Jo.

Jo I'm just saying.

John I know.

Jo I'm just saying.

(pause)

Do you want to see my bra?

John No. No, I didn't . . . no.

Jo I'm only going to show you a glimpse.

John Jo, I don't think that's the best thing.

Jo You so do. I can't believe how bad you are. You're naughty.

John Jo.

Jo It's a jungle bra.

John What do you mean it's a jungle bra?

Jo If you want to see it so bad you'll get your chance, John.

(She lifts her shirt up)

Do you think I have nice breasts?

(pause)

It's because it's camouflage that it's called a jungle bra.

(pause)

You have to look, John. To see it.

John Jo, maybe we should just be friends right now.

Jo Military is in, you know.

John Maybe stop showing me, OK?

Jo What's her name?

John Put your shirt down.

Jo What's her name?

John Put your shirt down.

(Jo drops her shirt)

It's Debbie.

Jo This is your girlfriend?

John Well, we're seeing each other.

Jo So she's your girlfriend.

John We're dating.

Jo Which makes her your girlfriend.

John I guess, yeah.

(pause)

Jo It's a nice name.

John What's wrong with Debbie?

Jo Nothing. It's a nice name.

John It's fine.

Jo Deb. You can shorten it to Deb, can't you?

John Yeah.

Jo Do you shorten it to Deb?

John Yeah, sometimes I do.

Jo Deb. Deb. Deb.

John I'm going to go back. I'm gonna see the others. You OK out here?

Jo Deb. Deb. Debbie.

Play no. 30

(A young daughter follows her mother around Debenhams in Weymouth. They look at towels)

Lilian Mum? You know our scales?

Kate Our bathroom scales?

Lilian Do you like them?

Kate I wouldn't say I like them. No one likes scales. I like them enough.

(pause)

Lilian Mum, would you say our scales are right all the time?

Kate What do you mean by right?

Lilian Like, when you get on them and the needle goes back and forth, and then it stops? Do you think it's right?

Kate Do you mean accurate, Lilian?

Lilian I mean accurate.

Kate Then you should say accurate. Yes, I think it's accurate.

Lilian Mum, could we maybe buy new scales in case our ones are getting old?

Kate They're not getting old. Your father bought them a couple of years ago.

Lilian It's just that there are ones that are digital now, and they're supposed to always be right. And accurate.

Kate We said you weren't to weigh yourself any more. They're not a toy.

Lilian Dad said I could.

Kate He's not saying you can any more.

Lilian Dad said I should watch myself.

Kate At your age we had things to do instead of weighing ourselves.

Lilian Mum, will I be obese?

Kate Don't be ridiculous.

Lilian How much is obese?

Kate It's a fat child.

Lilian How much is that?

Kate You have to be American to understand.

Lilian I think I'm going to be obese.

Kate You're a healthy girl who could be doing one or two more hockey practices each week if she expects to stay on the team. You're healthy.

Lilian Is that obese?

Kate Stop saying words you don't understand. I think we'll get the robin's egg towels. Pass that bathmat.

Lilian It would be nice to have blue scales, too. Matching scales. And ones that are digital.

Play no. 31

(A teenager sprawls on a seat on a bus in south London. She speaks quickly into a mobile)

It was the biggest whale tail I've ever seen ever. I thought Janelle was literally going to split her arse in half. It's, like, how much of your knickers do you have to show the entire world and all humanity? And she was just, like, picking things up off the floor, pencils, and bending over all day and her knickers were crawling up higher until basically there was more of her thong above her belt than, like, below. And Jerome says to me, 'Is that healthy?' and I was like, 'She is going to have the creepiest infection in less than thirty seconds,' and he was like, 'You say some of the funniest things in the world.'
(pause)
Who, Jerome? He's totally just a friend 'cos he fancies girls like Janelle, like he's always aware what Janelle's thong is doing at all times. He says it's minging but then he says, 'Look at where her thong is today,' and I'm like, 'If that thong is so minging, why you staring at it with the widest eyes of all humanity?' He says to me, 'You never wear thongs,' and I say, 'It's none of your business what is below my belt, Jerome, because I have the decency not to, like, floss my arse like Janelle every single day of the week, so often I bet she doesn't even wash her old thongs, just wears them again and again.' Jerome's all like, 'I

want to be with someone who has respect when it comes to their knickers,' and I was like, 'Hello, I'm right here.'

(pause)

No. Not out loud.

(pause)

'Cos he's a friend. It's just sad. Janelle is two years younger and she's, like, a different generation. She's a health risk, yeah? When I got my first thong, yeah? I would let just a bit of the fabric show, like a little piece of colour, just like the very end of a sunset or something. There was mystery back then, yeah? But it's over, isn't it? Janelle's ruined it. She's, like, ruined a piece of my childhood.

Play no. 32

(Two men stand in a pub in the City)

Dan They shouldn't interrupt.

Ed It's the first rule of sales.

Dan I would tell them, 'OK, mate, you've got DVDs to sell. They're illegal, so you've got to sell them in a restaurant, but be polite.'

Ed It's the only English word they know. DVD. DVD. DVD.

Dan And this isn't racism.

Ed No, you're not exactly the BNP.

Dan It's just politeness. I'm in favour of them. I've been on the Great Wall.

Ed We went to see the film.

Dan *The Crouching Tiger.*

Ed *The Crouching Dragon.*

Dan *The Crouching* . . .

Ed It was crouching.

Dan And I felt terrible when that cockle-picking thing happened.

Ed Get them into the cities.

Dan Exactly. That's not racist. It's just true. If there had been some sort of charity for them . . .

Ed They showed one on the telly.

Dan If it had been advertised better, I would have done something.

Ed A whip-round.

Dan I would at least have watched the ad.

Ed They say it so fast: DVD. DVD. DVD.

Dan It's just politeness, isn't it? They come at the worst times. Every time I'm eating with Jane.

Ed Maybe they've been sent by your wife.

Dan That's not very funny. Three dinners in with Jane and she's finally . . . I mean, we're finally sort of drunk enough. I'm going to ask her back to mine. She's going to say yes.

Ed DVD. DVD. DVD.

Dan Exactly. Out of nowhere. He's at the table with his little stack of them. Jane starts looking at DVDs. The moment's gone. We end up watching some Julia Roberts film. She falls asleep.

Ed Terrible.

Dan I mean, I'm not against foreigners.

Ed It's just politeness, isn't it?

Play no. 33

(A mother sits by her son's bedside in a Manchester hospital)

Lydia	This card from your auntie says, 'Turn that frown upside down.' Would you like to look at it?
Alex	No.
Lydia	I'll put it on your bedside table.
Alex	No.
Lydia	There's a little sun on the inside saying, 'Think sunny thoughts.'
Alex	Take it off the table, Mother.
Lydia	It's nice. I'll put it on the bed by your hand. How is your hand?
Alex	It's my wrist. It's not my hand.
Lydia	Of course.
	(pause)
	Some flowers in here would make it less dark. We want to remind you it's not winter for ever. Everyone's been very supportive.
Alex	Then you've told everyone . . .
Lydia	Just that you were a bit low.
Alex	And did you tell him?
Lydia	I thought it best to keep it in the family.
Alex	He's my partner.
Lydia	Stephen is not family.
Alex	He's my family.

Lydia He's not with you any more.

Alex I don't care – the note was to him.

Lydia But you didn't mean what you wrote.

(pause)

Now this card is from your sister. It says, 'Chin Up'. See, the man on it has a big chin.

Alex Did you even phone Stephen? Does he know where I am?

Lydia Would you like me to put your sister's card on the bedside table?

Alex No.

Lydia I guess we all get winter blues.

Alex Take it off the table, Mother.

Lydia According to Father Paul, what you're feeling is called SAD.

Alex Then you told Father Paul, did you? Just the family then?

Lydia He says light therapy works.

Alex I don't want light therapy.

Lydia We'll get you a good lightbulb.

Alex I'd like Stephen here.

Lydia Such a dark time of year. Sometimes I wonder why we live here.

Alex I know.

(pause)

Lydia Right. And this nice card here is from your gran.

Play no. 34

(Two builders in a van near Chepstow look at a Page 3 girl)

Harry That one? She's fit, she is.

Tim But do you see anything more?

Harry Nice set on her. Natural and all, if you like natural. Which I do.

Tim I'm not looking at those.

Harry I am. I'm a gentleman so natural's just fine with me.

Tim But look at her face.

Harry Since when am I supposed to look at the face?

Tim That isn't funny, yeah?

Harry All right, I'll look at her face. There. Decent face.

Tim It's all jokes to you, isn't it? All day it's having a laugh. Putting salt in my tea.

Harry I'm sorry, yeah?

Tim Calling me a bender if I drop something.

Harry I'm looking at her face now. OK? She's got a nose, a couple of eyes. I wouldn't kick her out of bed.

Tim Look closer.

Harry I'm not getting too close. Not to some girl from Bexley.

Tim Will you look into her eyes?

Harry What's the matter with you?

Tim Just don't make a joke and look into her eyes.

Harry We've got fifteen minutes left to eat. They're blue, those eyes. OK?

Tim What do you think they say about her?

Harry Do I care? You know there'll be another girl tomorrow, yeah? With eyes as well?

Tim I think she looks vulnerable.

Harry Do you now?

Tim There's something in her eyes.

Harry They treat them fine. They probably let her cover up right after the photo.

Tim I want to put clothes back on her.

Harry Bit late now mate.

Tim And give her, you know, dignity.

Harry Give her what?

(pause)

Tim Put this paper over her.

Harry Don't you tear up the football pages. I've not read those yet.

Tim I'm going to cover her.

Harry Then put your own Snickers over her, then. You happy now?

Tim She is.

Play no. 35

(Two nurses sit in a hospital canteen in Liverpool)

Linda Don't get me wrong, I like her.

Gail No one ever said you didn't.

Linda I've never said a word against her, or her culture, neither.

Gail She's got a lovely culture.

Linda Or the beads in her hair.

Gail They're part of her culture.

Linda Though they make a bit of a clacking sound when she leans over and all. And the older ones in the ward must think, 'Slow down, girl', what with her accent and all.

Gail It's her culture, speaking like that.

Linda They should bring nurses in from everywhere.

Gail They got all those doctors in Manchester from Malawi.

Linda Don't get me wrong – I like the girl. It's just hard when someone takes the good shifts.

Gail Oh, she does get a few good ones.

Linda She's always taking them. And I know she's got a long commute.

Gail She's on the bus for hours. But still, you know . . .

Linda I know it hasn't been easy.

Gail With the family back there.

Linda But still. No word of a lie, I says to her, 'I've worked here for six years.'

Gail Did you say that to her?

Linda I says to her, 'Excuse me, I've worked here nearly seven years.' Seniority counts.

Gail It's about time someone said something to her.

Linda I like the girl, but she takes the holidays she wants.

Gail We were all set on Croatia, too. Couldn't go because of her.

Linda I says to her, 'It's lovely your children had never seen snow.'

Gail Oh, that was touching, wasn't it?

Linda Don't get me wrong, it's lovely they got to ski. But there's seniority . . .

Gail Maybe not in her culture.

Linda I says, 'You'd better watch yourself.' Don't get me wrong, I like her.

Gail Of course. We all do.

Linda But there's seniority . . .

Play no. 36

(A mother and daughter stand at a bus stop in Tooting, south London)

Lila	Your father will speak to her again someday.
Gita	Except he said to her 'I'll never speak to you again.' Loudly.
Lila	But he said that to Uncle, too.
Gita	And Uncle died without having another conversation with him. His own brother.
Lila	It's different with a daughter.
Gita	Except he said to her 'You're not my daughter.' Loudly.
Lila	No. He said 'You're no daughter of mine.'
Gita	Is there a difference, Mum?
Lila	A small one. He needs time. He's hurt.
Gita	She's hurt. She's done nothing wrong.
Lila	You've always known about this man your sister is with?
Gita	Of course.
Lila	Even when I was introducing her to suitable Indian boys? That one from Wolverhampton drove down.
Gita	He was awful.
Lila	He drove down in his own car. How long has she been with this one?
Gita	He has a name, you know. Andy. Andrew.
Lila	I don't like Andyandrew. That's not a good name.
Gita	Andy or Andrew. They've been together ten years.
Lila	And she has never said a single word to us?

Gita She couldn't. He's good to her.

Lila So was the boy from Wolverhampton. And suitable.

Gita Andrew wanted to meet Daddy. He wanted to speak to him.

Lila Your sister was always going to hurt her father.

Gita Not true.

Lila And now you are both getting so old.

Gita Thanks, Mum.

Lila I wanted two good marriages.

Gita Well, you've got two successful daughters.

Lila Now I'll only have one good marriage, won't I?

Gita That's the thing. It's probably time for you to meet my David.

Lila Who is David?

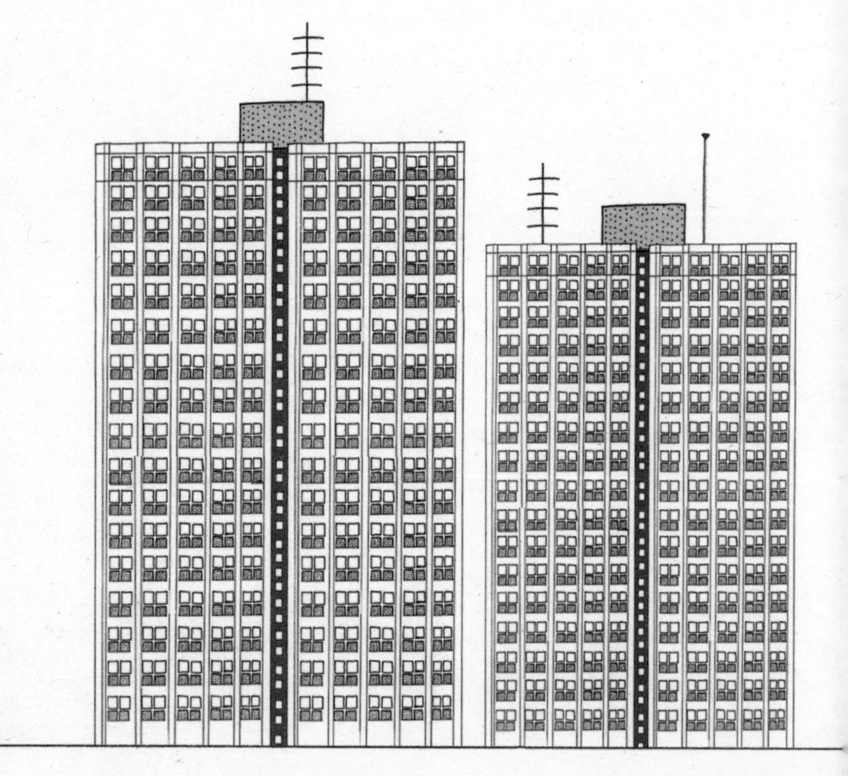

Play no. 37

(A daughter helps her mother into a black cab in central London)

Joy Fine. Fine. It was a perfectly adequate group of ladies.
Deb And Agnes was there.
Joy Agnes was fine. I've never had a problem with that woman.
Deb And you made amends with Elsie.
Joy Elsie apologised before the trip.
Deb Then was it the coach, Mum? Was it uncomfortable?
Joy I can endure a coach.
Deb We paid for one of the best companies. That's what they said.
Joy I was sat near the toilet.
Deb But you were excited to see the art of Berlin.
Joy In theory.
Deb You planned the trip, you have the book.
Joy I know, I have the catalogue.
Deb We bought it for you.
Joy It's just the trip felt very German.
Deb Mum, we have no problem with Germany now.
Joy I thought of all the young English men I knew, and your father.
Deb We have to move past that.
Joy He was appalled when you bought that Volkswagen.
Deb That was thirty years ago.
Joy It was just a colourful little bug to you, wasn't it? Not to us.
Deb Why don't we arrange it so you don't have a seat by the loo.

Joy You thought you could just buy a Volkswagen, didn't you?

Deb Fine.

(pause)

You could take the train back and meet the coach tour in Paris.

Joy I don't know about that.

Deb Is there something wrong with the tour?

Joy No, it's just it's very French, isn't it?

Deb You like French food.

Joy The people are very . . . there was all the collaboration, of course.

Deb OK. Well, you're welcome to come on holiday with us.

Joy Oh, I don't want to infringe on your holiday.

Deb We could rent a larger villa.

Joy This was meant to be your anniversary trip, wasn't it?

Deb Something like that.

Joy I don't want to be a burden. I'll come, but only if I'm not a burden.

Play no. 38

(Two teens in a McDonalds in Swansea. They wear eyeliner)

Sam It was so easy to see it had been, like, messed with. I always hide it under my bed.

Evan Had it been moved?

Sam It was so obvious they'd been reading it. You can practically see their fingerprints.

Evan Have they been reading your blog too?

Sam Every day.

Evan My parents too. I can check their computer to see the websites they've been to.

Sam I can check which songs my dad is secretly listening to on my laptop.

Evan Why are they, like, the worst ever at snooping about?

Sam He was listening to an old Cannibal Corpse album. It's right there on my screen.

Evan Mine was listening to my Napalm Death. Like you can even hear the lyrics.

Sam They're looking for hints. Then Mum's saying 'Are you OK?' so much.

Evan Yeah. 'You're important to us. We love you.' All the we love yous.

Sam Like fifty we love yous a day.

Evan The weird thing is I didn't even know the girl.

Sam I didn't know her either. She was a year below.

(pause)

Evan But did you read that last post on her MySpace?

Sam The one about the pain ending?

Evan They took it down before I saw it.

Sam It was all about wanting to switch off the pain. Something about stepping out into something quiet and painless.

Evan Some people can make it sound so much, like, a good decision. Do you know what I mean?

Sam You want these chips?

Evan You can have them.

(pause)

Sam Do you ever think about doing it?

Evan Once or twice.

Sam I did once. But you know what I thought? I've only ever been to gigs when Dad's been waiting outside in the car.

Evan Not Obituary.

Sam We got picked up after Obituary by my dad. Imagine ending your life like that.

Evan Not seeing Camden.

Sam Not seeing, like, Helgrind without Dad waiting outside in the car.

Evan And never drinking beer in a park in London.

Sam To Camden, on the street with two tins each.

Evan I don't know what she got. She didn't get to see Camden in her life.

Sam Do you want more chips?

Evan I think it's worth holding on, yeah? There's more to it all.

Sam More than Swansea?

Evan I think it gets better. Maybe not peaceful but, like, a bit better.

Play no. 39

(A sales assistant speaks to a customer in a shop in Glasgow)

. . . Oh, I know. And for shoes I can recommend at least seven places. So yeah, it's a lot different around here. Changes. Yeah. Apparently they used to make . . .
(pause)
. . . boats here? Ships.

Play no. 40

(An elderly man stands in front of his GP in his surgery in King's Lynn)

Aidan Sorry, sorry, I'm so sorry. You weren't waiting an entire hour, were you?

Ed About fifty-five minutes, it was.

Aidan Well, that's not an hour, is it? You can see we're a little behind.

Ed I was the first patient.

Aidan But we're behind from this morning, you see? Understand? Could you hold on a moment? It's really not easy for me on a day like this.

Ed It's not easy for me to wee right now.

Aidan Right. That's fine. Right. Then let's have a look at the flexibility?

Ed The flexibility of what?

Aidan Of your knee.

Ed I didn't say knee.

Aidan OK. That's . . . wonderful. Fine.

(pause)

I'm sorry, I was just checking something else. Sorry, Mr Hilton. Now, your knee?

Ed It's not my knee. I'm not Mr Hilton.

Aidan Of course you're not. I'm just . . . Oh, I see. Little mistake. I'm writing on hotel stationery.

Ed That won't do for a prescription.

Aidan No. Could I borrow a pen? The pens they give us have no ink. Please sit down. I'm so, so sorry.

Ed I said I can't sit down. That's the problem.

Aidan Of course. Sorry, sorry. Our computer's been down. These NHS computers.

Ed I can tell you the problem in my own words.

Aidan Well, it should be on this computer. Someone's got coffee on the keyboard. Now then. Some urine perhaps?

Ed I did that a few minutes ago.

Aidan And how did that go, urine-wise?

Ed I gave the full container to you. It's all very painful these days.

Aidan You gave the urine back to me, did you?

Ed I'm worried about this. About relapsing.

Aidan And the urine? Did you notice where I put it?

Ed Over that side of your desk.

Aidan Past the sandwich? So it's got to be either this vial or this one?

Ed I only filled out one.

Aidan I'm sorry. We're very busy. Would you be able to recognise the colour? Mr . . . Hilton?

Play no. 41

(In a park in north London two teenagers look at a knife)

Leon It's got them little ridges in the blade.

Sean That's wicked, yeah? Five of them.

Leon Six. For cutting through everything.

Sean It's well dangerous.

Leon I cut an apple this morning. It was like: did I just cut something? It was that smooth.

Sean Whose apple was it?

Leon My mum's or whatever. She's on about fruit now.

Sean It's all that five a day, yeah?

Leon And I was like, five a day with a knife in it.

Sean Check the grip on it.

Leon The grip is so you can grip and twist.

Sean Imagine getting it deep into, like, a watermelon. That would be sick.

Leon Or into him.

Sean So, that mean you still want to do it then?

Leon It's why I got the blade, yeah? It's like all four of us planned. It's a plan now, yeah?

Sean But the other two are gone.

Leon Then it's a smaller plan but it's a plan. Gimme your finger.

Sean No.

Leon I'll show you what the tip can do.

(pause)

Sean That's a way longer blade than what I thought.

Leon Yeah, three times in and out. That's all you need to do.

Sean I didn't think it was gonna be like that.

Leon You scared of it?

Sean I'm not that scared of it.

Leon You think we have a choice?

Sean It's just I never expected it to be all, like, real and sharp.

Leon You heard what he said to you? That kind of disrespect?

Sean I know. But . . .

Leon That kind of shit?

Sean That was once though.

Leon I'm only doing this for you. Him saying all that right to your face? It's like, what else is going to teach him?

Sean It's heavy, too. Feel it.

Leon What were you expecting, yeah?

Sean I don't know. It's all just way heavier than I thought.

Play no. 42

(A cab driver speaks to a passenger in Bristol)

Ed	Yeah, me too. I always say you keep arguments at home. Don't make a scene in public.
Chris	That's what I was taught.
Ed	We think the same, then, you and I. Peas in a pod.
Chris	And here I am basically crying. I'm sorry.
Ed	No, mate. When mine did it to me I was all tears. A bloke my size trying not to cry in a restaurant? Not pretty.
Chris	This was your wife?
Ed	Ex-wife. The second she told me she became my ex.
Chris	Because it's betrayal, isn't it?
Ed	The split second she said that other bloke's name. And he was a friend. And he was a City supporter.
Chris	It's worse when the man's a friend.
Ed	Mate, no, it's a slap in the face. From both of them.
Chris	This man had been a good friend to us.
Ed	Now he's gone and wrecked it. He wrecks it and she's an ex in record time.
Chris	And you feel like such a fool sitting there.
Ed	Know what? She said it to me with a bit of glee, know what I mean?
Chris	Like they enjoy twisting the knife.
Ed	Not even twisting. Deep in, right through me, and I ain't small.

Chris You're not exactly huge.

Ed You're kind. I never told someone this before but you and me, mate, we're the same. I couldn't throw away my wedding ring. Told everyone I buried it in a field. I got it right here. Never leaves me.

Chris I'll throw mine into the sea in Brighton.

Ed Is that where you were married?

Chris It's where I first met Brian.

Ed And who's Brian, then?

Chris My husband. Or I guess ex-husband now.

Ed Oh. So . . . Right then.

Chris But thank you. To know it happens to other men.

Ed Well, yeah.

Chris I'm happy you could tell that to me.

Ed Well. Sure. But it's not exactly the same thing, is it?

Chris Because I'm going to get rid of my ring?

Ed No. My ring means a different thing. It's a woman's ring. Not saying you all shouldn't . . . you know. But . . .

Chris This is me. On the left. Before the lights.

Play no. 43

(An elderly churchgoer speaks to his vicar in a church in rural Suffolk)

Archie Those people? Oh, no, no, no. Certainly not.

Henry I've seen them in the village, though.

Archie Well, they don't live in the village.

Henry They have a home here.

Archie They have a house here, that's for certain. It's the Old Manse, you know.

Henry And I've seen them drive through the village on a few occasions.

Archie They do drive through it. They've got a very large car.

Henry I think it would be lovely to see them at a service on Sunday.

Archie Well, they're from London.

Henry Fine, but they still might be interested in the local church.

Archie They're from London, though. They only come here for the weekends, and sometimes not even that.

Henry But, you see, our services do happen to be on Sunday.

Archie I've not once seen them down at the pub, not even when the pub started with all that new food.

Henry Would you have a word with these people?

Archie I did once. A few words, it was.

Henry Would you mind giving them a welcome?

Archie They sort of keep themselves to themselves, you see. I'm sure they'd rather see your face.

Henry Fine. I do, however, have my other five parishes to see to.

Archie We're all busy around here, you know.

Henry I understand you're very busy.

Archie I was just strimming round the headstones in the churchyard. I know the villagers out there, don't I? They'd be happy to come to a service if they could.

Henry Fine, then. How many people were in the congregation today?

Archie There was me. There was you, of course.

Henry And just Mrs Wilton.

Archie She comes mostly just to see another living soul, poor old girl.

Henry She looked happy today though.

Archie Oh, sure she is. She just can't hear a word you say.

Henry Right. Then I feel it's our duty to make some of the newcomers welcome.

Archie Wait till the Christmas service, then. I seem to recall them attending that one.

Play no. 44

(A young woman and her parents sit in a restaurant in east London)

Jo	You finishing your pizza, Mum?
Dad	Your mother and I will eat when we get home.
Jo	Fine. Great. I'm so glad this has ruined the afternoon.
Dad	We're just shaken.
Jo	Mum, it didn't mean anything.
Mum	We're not used to being on the underground.
Jo	It's obviously more than just the underground.
Dad	Your mother got worried. I got worried. With all these bombings, it could happen in any carriage.
Jo	All these bombings . . .? Dad, it was one kid reading a book.
Dad	A book that said 'Preparation for Jihad' on the front page.
Jo	It was a kid being provocative. He was holding it for anyone to see. He didn't even turn the page. It didn't mean anything.
Dad	And that woman beside him, completely covered except for the eyes.
Jo	So what? They weren't together.
Dad	They were sitting together.
Jo	Until they got off at different stops.
Dad	I find that whole outfit sinister. It's a mask. I don't wear a mask in public.
Jo	So now I'm Jack Straw's daughter.
Dad	It's a valid objection to make.

Jo Enjoy your marriage to Jack Straw, Mum. The two of you. You could at least take off your coats. Your big jihad isn't going to happen at Pizza Express.
(pause)

Mum We're sorry. We'll eat a proper meal together soon.

Jo I know, Mum. I know that.

Mum How are the capers on your pizza?

Jo Fine, Mum.

Mum Do you like capers now?

Jo I guess. Sure.

Mum Just because the village pub has a pizza oven now. They do one with capers. It's all changed. All new. And do you remember the Duncans' daughter? A year younger than you.

Jo She moved back.

Mum She came home. She said it was such a relief to leave the city. All the trouble. Like today. To be in her community again. She's very happy.

Jo I'm sure she is.

Mum Very. She asks about you.

Jo I don't really know her.

Mum She was wondering whether you're thinking of leaving the city.

Jo I'm going to get the bill.

Play no. 45

(A young couple look at the for-sale notices in an estate agent's window in south London)

Jack I don't know exactly how. Maybe by reading police reports?

Emily And then what? Waiting for it to go on the market?

Jack It could be worth it.

Emily Do they clean up all the . . .

Jack Of course. It's like a normal home.

Emily How would that affect the price?

Jack A murder must take off at least £15,000.

Emily Even with that we couldn't have a study.

Jack Well, not in zone two.

Emily What about something worse than a murder?

Jack Like one of those dungeons?

Emily How far would that take the price down?

Jack You wouldn't be able to buy it for years. And they usually tear down houses like that.

Emily Thing is, I don't know if I'd want to live in a place like that.

Jack And you don't get that sort of thing happening so much in zone two.

Emily I just don't think reading police reports is a reliable system. *(pause)*

Jack Is there still any bomb damage anywhere?

Emily From the Second World War?

Jack I just thought there might be a place they haven't fixed . . .

Emily Or some more recent bombings?

Jack You know, Christine was on the ladder when she was twenty-six.

Emily We'll be on the ladder.

Jack If you're not on the ladder by thirty, it's not worth getting near the ladder.

Emily We haven't missed our chance.

Jack The ladder is right there, though. It needs to happen.

Emily Maybe it's OK not to be on it, given the climate and all.

Jack Brian's on it, too.

Emily He's thirty. It's fine.

Jack But he completed about two weeks before his birthday.

Emily It's OK. Maybe there will be a murder. In a house near a park.

Play no. 46

(A young daughter sits next to her father in First Class on a train to Birmingham)

Lily	Five more stops, Dad.
Dad	Four more stops, Lily.
Lily	And then home.
Dad	And bed for you.
Lily	I'm glad we came to this seat.
Dad	Me, too. We can't stay for long.
Lily	My legs were getting sore.
Dad	And you tell me if you see the ticket collector. Right away.
Lily	It was so noisy where we were.
Dad	People pay more for this quiet.
Lily	Did we pay more for this quiet?
	(pause)
Dad	No. But we paid for a seat. It's good to be sitting down.
Lily	Can we sit here for four more stops?
Dad	We're only here because the rest of the train is full. I'm not having you standing.
Lily	Why is it full?
Dad	Because they overbooked. Again.
Lily	But there's loads of seats here.
Dad	It's different.
Lily	But we were just on the other side of the door.

Dad This is First Class.

Lily Why don't all the standing people come and sit here?

Dad Because it's not for them.

Lily Is it for better people?

Dad No.

Lily Is that man First Class?

Dad You don't have to point at him.

Lily This table's made of real wood.

Dad It doesn't make it a better table.

Lily And they get a free biscuit.

Dad Then stick it in your pocket, if you want.

Lily Do you think Mum would have sat here with us?

Dad No. She didn't like First Class.

Lily Because she was noisy, too?

Dad No, she just thought it was wrong.

Lily She thought a lot of things were wrong. The seat's nice, though.

Dad It doesn't make it a better seat.

Lily Are you First Class, Dad?

Dad In some ways. Only in some ways.

Play no. 47

(An older man checks in at Heathrow Airport)

Joe	I've got my whole life here in these bags.
Becca	Big trip then?
Joe	I'm a mule, a pack mule.
Becca	And if I could just see your ticket.
Joe	Whip me with a cane, says the mule. Whip me on the behind.
Becca	I'll just take that ticket from you.
Joe	I'm going to live with my daughter.
Becca	I'm sure that will be nice. I'm just checking availability.
Joe	It won't be nice. She's been in America twenty-five years. She's a small, worried American now.
Becca	It's lovely when families are reunited.
Joe	It's only because I broke my ankle. She leaves all these bloody messages all day on the answerphone. She sounds like my bank manager.
Becca	And did you happen to pack your passport in all of that?
Joe	Yes. I'm sorry I can't read your nametag without my glasses.
Becca	Becca.
Joe	Becca. Lovely. Don't laugh at the photograph, Becca.
Becca	And did you pack your own luggage today?
Joe	Yes. All these bloody tablets. Four messages about my tablets. Don't forget, she says.
Becca	Have you left your luggage unattended at any time?

Joe	No. You are a Mediterranean beauty. Your parents are Spanish, aren't they?
Becca	Not exactly Spanish. A bit further east. Now here's your boarding pass.
Joe	Then it's goodbye to England, isn't it?
Becca	You'll be back. A healthy fellow like yourself.
Joe	I have to be in good shape to carry all this. My whole life. Like a pack mule with all my belongings around me? A Jew in one of those war movies, aren't I?
Becca	I'm sorry?
Joe	Have you ever seen those films? I could be in *Schindler's List*. *(pause)*
Becca	Next.
Joe	Is that goodbye then? Wish me luck?
Becca	Next.

Play no. 48

(Two people sit at the back of a night bus making its way towards Finsbury Park, London. It is two in the morning. He has a French accent. Hers is American. His arm is around her shoulders)

Ashley So it wasn't a real stroke. Or it wasn't a crippling stroke. Do you know what a stroke is?

Marcel Yes.

Ashley I don't know how to say it in French.

Marcel Yes.

Ashley Un mal de . . .

Marcel Yes, I know what it is.

Ashley Well, it wasn't a major one but it was still, you know . . .

Marcel It was a stroke.

Ashley And when my dad phoned I could just tell it was trouble. First of all, they never call me past ten at night. They're both very aware when it comes to different timezones, with me being so far ahead.

Marcel France is even further.

Ashley France is what?

Marcel In my country we are later. We are one hour forward.

Ashley Well, England is, like, five hours later than Baltimore, so I knew something was up. You get that feeling in your throat. And you know when your father comes on the phone – I don't know if this has ever happened to you – but your father comes on the phone and he sounds like someone else?

Marcel You look beautiful.

Ashley And . . .

Marcel In this light.

Ashley . . . and your dad. Sorry?

Marcel I was worried that when we got outside the club you wouldn't be as beautiful as you were inside. Not so. This bus does not have good light, but you are still beautiful.

Ashley Thanks.

Marcel Your hair.

Ashley That's sweet. That's really. So . . . but . . . so my dad. Sorry to go back to this.

Marcel No, no, no.

Ashley My dad told me that Mom had been making strange noises in the night, moving the sheets, that kind of thing. When he woke up she was having a stroke. Or she had just had it.

Marcel We are three stops from my house right now.

Ashley And. And so he got her to the hospital as fast as he could, which was lucky because our car? It's a wonder anyone can even drive the thing with its back end almost ninety per cent rusted off. My dad walks everywhere now because we've only been at this new house for six months. He's all about walking. It used to be biking but then he was like 'No, you can only begin to understand a city if you walk its streets.' That kind of thing. So it was just lucky that when he turned the ignition the car actually started. He drove there as fast as he could.

Marcel Is she dead?

Ashley No, it was just a small stroke. A petit . . .

Marcel This was your mother who had the stroke?

Ashley Yes.

Marcel And your father is black?

Ashley Yes.

Marcel And your mother is white?

Ashley Yes. And, you know, her recovery has just been amazing. She did the whole walking on a treadmill, the whole physical therapy thing. Her face after it happened was twisted. It was like the nerve endings had been damaged. But somehow she's really improved it through exercises and she looks, I'd say, about ninety-five per cent as good as she looked before. If you knew her before you might be able to tell, but it's not like people stare.

Marcel Why do they stare?

Ashley No, they don't stare. She's recovered.

Marcel And are your parents able to hold hands in public?

Ashley Oh, they're totally affectionate. I've been so proud of my dad, how he's handled it? Out of all my friends' parents I'd say eighty per cent are divorced. So my parents are in the minority. But they're so in love, so there for each other, kissing at the table, that kind of stuff, which is kind of weird when it's people that age. But you know what's really weird? The only lasting effect of the stroke is that my mom will just forget easy words for things around her. Like the water will be running in the sink? And she'll say, 'Turn off the . . .' And she'll point at it and sort of shake her finger at it, and I'll be like, 'Mom, do you mean the faucet?' And she'll say, 'Yes, the faucet.' That kind of stuff happens all the time, and I know it's got something to do with the stroke.

Marcel I love your black skin.

Ashley	And . . . sorry?
Marcel	I love the way it gets darker around your wrinkles. Around your eyes you are very black.
Ashley	Thanks.
Marcel	We are two more stops from my house now. It is up this hill. That's the park over there I told you about. And that is the store where I do my shopping. It's owned by Arabs. *(pause)*
Ashley	So, I mean, not to keep dwelling on this. I guess what I meant to say is that my mother is OK. But it just makes you think how precious life is. And how . . .
Marcel	You've heard of The Strokes, right?
Ashley	The what?
Marcel	A band. They are called The Strokes. Just because you were mentioning strokes one second ago.
Ashley	I guess I've heard of them.
Marcel	They are very popular.
Ashley	I don't even, you know, have a stereo over here.
Marcel	I have a Sony stereo. The new Strokes CD is very good. You will like them. I am going to play two of their songs for you when we get to my place. Number five is very fast. Number one is slower. I think number five is better but it will be interesting to hear what you say. Is that fine? *(pause)* Do you think that's fine?
Ashley	Sure.
Marcel	Do you like rock and roll?
Ashley	Yeah, I sort of like everything.
Marcel	Or do you like rap music all the time?

Play no. 49

(An anti-animal testing demonstration table in Manchester. It is covered with laminated photographs. A young man walks up and begins to look at the pamphlets. He wears a T-shirt emblazoned with an image of an alien smoking a joint)

Tim — Are these real?

David — The photos of the animals? Yes, they're all real.

Tim — What, is that a cat?

David — It's a monkey. You see, this is what happens when animals are experimented on. We haven't changed or altered the photos in any way.

Tim — They take their faces off like that?

David — It's all in this literature. If you're interested in monkeys, I can tell you, for instance, that polio researchers were mistaken for years because of testing on monkeys. There's no need for it.

Tim — That's crazy.

David — It's why we feel it's important to be here.

Tim — That one's got no face, that cat.

David — That's actually the monkey.

Tim — What, a monkey?

David — It's something to remember when your wife or girlfriend is buying cosmetics.

Tim — I don't have a girlfriend.
(pause)

Tim Who took this one? Is that with a zoom?

David We've had volunteers who went undercover at the testing facilities.

Tim With a zoom lens?

David Perhaps.

Tim I'd like to see the model number of that zoom. Is that a cat?

David That's a monkey.

Tim That's a monkey? That's crazy. That one there's like Hellraiser. It's wicked you can show this stuff on the street.

David Can I interest you in signing the petition?

Tim I guess. Good prizes?

David No, it's a petition.

Tim For the photos?

David No, the photos are a way of bringing attention to the issue. The issue is animal testing. We're collecting signatures because we feel . . .

Tim Is that one a rabbit?

David Yes.

Tim Is that a rabbit? Fucking hell. That is well disgusting. Did it die after that? I bet it died like minutes after the photo.

David A lot of them do die.

Tim You can tell with that one because basically it's got no skin except for that bit there. I once seen that done to a squirrel. It could have gone on your board it was that good. It was still alive until my brother started cutting its belly.

David We're against animal cruelty so I don't really want to hear about that. Please, it's very easy to sign.

Tim My brother? If he was going to sign it, he'd put down a fake name probably.

David If you'd like to put down your own name it would be appreciated.

Tim So how long have you been involved in this, mate?

David I'm quite new. I've been brought along to get signatures.

Tim Do you process the photos?

David No.

Tim Because most places, my brother says, they won't even develop stuff like this. But then it doesn't really matter with digital.

(He points to the other person working the table)

Is that your girlfriend?

David Yes, well, Samantha is actually my wife. She got me into this.

Tim She must take the photos.

David No. We have people all over.

Tim So what do I get if I sign the petition?

David Just, I don't know, the feeling that you're doing good in the world. Sam?

(Samantha leans over)

What does someone get for signing the petition?

Samantha Hello, there. Well, they get personal satisfaction.

David That's what I said.

Samantha Then I've trained you well, haven't I?

(She laughs. It is a strong laugh)

Tim She's trained you well. I like that. She's trained you. I like her.

Samantha You should see what I do when he gets out of line.

Tim What, does she peel your skin off?

David No.

Tim	Like that cat?
David	No. And that is, as I said, a monkey.
Tim	I like how she said you were well trained. Will she train anyone else?
David	No.
Tim	Like me?
David	Are you interested in animal rights?
Tim	I'm interested in animals, yeah. I'm not a vegetarian, if that's what you mean. I suppose I have to give you my debit card details?
David	No, no, we're not looking for money. Just a signature.
Tim	This one is such an intense photo. It's too bad.
David	It's more than too bad, frankly. All of this – everything you see here – is an indication of a societal ill.
Tim	No, it's like I would have shot it from above. I wanted to get that whale in the Thames from above. I got one brilliant one when it looked really sick. That would have been good to put up in your display.
David	You see, that's not animal testing.
Tim	Have you ever put out a photo of, like, a horse without any skin?
David	No.
Tim	Mate, if you had a banner of it up here, above the table, of a horse kind of stretched out and without skin. I think it would be very effective. You could see it from across the street. Or do you have a picture of two rabbits hanging without skin?
David	We don't choose. This is what happens in the world, what is happening, why we're fighting.
Tim	I bet there's a horse picture somewhere.

David	Well, I really bet there isn't.
Tim	Well, maybe you can ask.
David	Samantha is busy and sorry, all we're really looking for here is a signature.
Tim	*(to Samantha)* Excuse me.
David	I'll ask her. I will ask her.
Samantha	Are you scaring people away, David? Are you badgering people, you little badger?
David	No, no.
Tim	You'll have to train him some more.
Samantha	He's quite a well-trained little badger.
David	This gentleman was curious about photos of other animals.
Tim	Of a horse.
Samantha	There are no horses. Why is that? Do you know of any horses being mistreated? *(pause)*
Tim	Yes.
Samantha	This is sometimes how we learn. Make sure you leave a contact number for David.
Tim	I know of a horse being abused because my brother . . .?
Samantha	I'm sure he's witnessed something horrible. Leave your number and I'll make sure we're in touch. And thank you. *(She turns away)*
Tim	You should see what my brother did to a horse. That could go on your table too.
David	I really don't have much time to spend, so I'm going to have to ask you for the signature, and if not . . . I mean you're welcome to read, quietly, the material.
Tim	Or we make a deal.

David	We don't, you see, pay people for signatures. We just hope you see an injustice and feel obliged to act against it.
Tim	For photos?
David	Sorry?
Tim	For just a small one.
	(pause)
	Can I ask Sam?
David	No, no you can't ask Samantha.
Tim	Has she trained you to be a helpful badger?
	(pause)
David	We have these.
Tim	That's the pamphlet everyone gets. Is that one there a photo of a rabbit?
David	Yes.
Tim	It's really horrible.
David	Yes.
Tim	But then you sort of can't stop looking at it.
	(pause. David rolls it up and hands it to him)
Samantha	So what do we have to do to get you to sign? This little badger's got to get back to work. What's that?
David	Nothing.
Tim	I'll make sure I tell you about the horse, Sam. Do I sign right here?
David	Yes.
Tim	Would you like my middle name as well as my number?
David	No.
Tim	I can give you my middle name as well.
David	No.
Tim	It's not a problem.
David	I really don't want to know. Your middle name.

Play no. 50

(A man and his girlfriend order
in a late-night kebab shop in Portsmouth)

Ed	Chicken and chips, yeah? Then chips, portion of chips, chips, chips and pitta and what? Burger and chips for Tooley?
Stace	He wanted chips with it, too.
Ed	I ordered it with chips, yeah? Another chips then.
Adnan	Please slow down.
Ed	Am I not speaking English? And what you want Stace?
Stace	I'm going to be sick.
Adnan	Not in the shop, please. No sick in the shop.
Ed	Save it till we get out, Stace. Just save it.
Stace	A bit came up, though.
Ed	I'm not queuing again, am I? Just save it.
Adnan	No sick in the shop, please.
Ed	Yeah, we understand English, all right? What does Stevie want?
Stace	He's being sick right now.
Ed	But after that.
Stace	Chips with chicken, he said.
Ed	In a pitta, or what? I'm not a mind reader.
Adnan	That's another portion of chips, then?
Ed	Am I not speaking English to you? Chips, yeah? Chicken and chips, chips, chips, portion of onion.
Stace	I'm not having a portion of onion.

Ed Onion baji with garlic sauce, is what I said.

Adnan And what sauce on the chips?

Ed Yeah. Exactly. And another portion of chips. And did Heather want chips?

Stace Were you dancing with Heather?

Ed What? What you on about?

Stace When I was getting drinks. You were dancing with her.

Ed She was just nearby.

Adnan Garlic sauce on everything?

Stace Why you buying chips for Heather if you weren't dancing with her?

Ed It's one portion of chips.

Stace Why aren't you buying me chips?

Ed 'Cos you're being sick in your mouth.

Stace You could at least buy me chips as a sign, instead of her.

Ed And waste a portion?

Stace It's what it means, yeah? You don't even know what chips means.

Adnan Any drinks with that?

Stace Fine. Give chips to her, then. Give her all your chips. Fine.

Play no. 51

(A small park in north London. Two men are picking up rubbish with their metal implements. They are dressed in reflective council vests)

Pete So you come across lots of unopened bottles, don't you?

Phil Bottles. Loads of tins.

Pete You ever take them?

Phil The tins once in a while.

Pete You serious?

Phil If they've still got the labels on. You could end up with mangoes if you don't.

Pete Yeah, or maybe there's some madman who puts, like, his shit in a tin.

Phil Never seen that.

Pete I'd just rather buy my tins in the shop.

(They sift through the rubbish. Phil uncovers a bottle of Budweiser beer. The cap is still on)

Pete Budweiser's not bad, yeah?

Phil When you got nothing else.

Pete No, I used to drink it when I was with my brother in America. They slam it there. My brother slams lager.

Phil They treat it like a soft drink. It's just Pepsi to them.

Pete You can buy it in cases of ninety.

Phil And tasteless too, it's so gassy.

Pete You want it?

Phil No.

Pete The label's on it.

Phil I didn't say I take everything with a label, did I?

Pete All right.

Phil There's discretion, yeah?

(pause)

Pete It's sort of disgusting. This job? If you think about it.

Phil You get the odd diamond.

Pete Tell me when you see one.

(pause)

Phil I play this game sometimes where I try to work out where a piece of rubbish comes from. Because everything has its own story. That's just my own personal motto. Everything in here was once somewhere else. When you think of it that way the whole job gets more interesting.

Pete Gets interesting how?

Phil You should give it a try.

(Pete picks up a newspaper with his metal implement)

Pete What was this in the beginning? A newspaper? What's it now? A wet newspaper. You're right. That's really interesting.

Phil You're not even trying. What about this?

Pete I've never seen an empty packet of crisps before. That's absolutely stunning.

Phil But if you were playing the game, you'd be able to imagine that maybe this packet of crisps belonged to some kid who might become the, I don't know, the next Frank Sinatra.

Pete The next what?

Phil Or whoever. It's just an example. Just using it as an example.

Pete But it didn't even belong to them. He just used it for a few minutes, or however long it takes to eat a packet of crisps. It's not like it was one of his things.

Phil Who truly knows what we remember later on?

Pete You remember every packet of crisps you've eaten, then?

Phil No, but I'll be having a laugh at you in twenty years when some young singer is on the telly and he's talking about how his dad would take him to the park . . .

Pete And buy him a bag of crisps?

Phil Sure.

Pete And when have you seen a singer on telly talk about what kind of crisps he used to eat when he was small and sitting in a park? You've been going through the bins too long mate.

Phil You find the odd diamond, you do.

(He retrieves a tissue spotted with blood)

Pete Oh, come on. It's a bloody tissue.

Phil But what do you think its story is?

Pete Someone had a nosebleed. I'm not touching it.

Phil But if we were playing the game.

Pete We're not playing the game.

Phil But if you gave the game a chance.

Pete We're not playing the game.

(pause)

Phil I'll tell you what I see. I see a terrorist, yeah? Muslim, yeah? But he wants to go straight. So he says to his terrorist mates. 'Listen, boys.' He's saying this in . . . that other language. 'Listen, fellas. I can't do this. I thought I was a killer. I'm not a killer. I thought I wanted to ruin society. I don't want to ruin society.' So one of his other terrorist mates comes walking over to him. And bam, right in the face. He goes running out of the flat, you know, their hideout. His face is a mess, blood everywhere, but he's got this tissue in his pocket.

Pete What are you? Jeffrey fucking Archer? It's a tissue with some blood on it. It's from some pathetic drug addict . . .

Phil OK. That works too. That's the idea.

Pete The idea of what?

Phil Go on. So what about this addict. Is it a man? Woman? Maybe she shoots up twice a day?

Pete There's no story. It's a thing.

Phil She's got two kids by different fathers and she can't support them so she's out on the street whispering to all the men passing by.

Pete Yeah. She says 'Watch out for the man picking up rubbish. He says he works for the Council but he's really a nutcase.'

Phil OK. Sure. I'd happily play a part. Sure.

Pete Put the tissue back, Philip.

Phil Don't point your implement at me, Peter.

Pete I really, on a day like this, don't need to be standing here acting out the life history of a bloody tissue. It's not going to make me feel better.

Phil You see how it passes the time, though? You see that?

Pete You know what else passes the time. Doing work.

Phil Doing work.

(They eventually begin picking up more rubbish around the bin. Phil lifts out a baggy of powder)

'Meanwhile the terrorists back at the flat kept producing their anthrax powder.'

Pete Oh, that's it.

Phil 'But one packet was missing. The good terrorist had slipped it into his pocket in the confusion before he ran away. Out on the street he had to hide it somewhere.'

(Pete throws his implement to the ground)

I'm sorry.

Pete There's a reason . . .

Phil That was uncalled for.

Pete There's a reason it's called rubbish, yeah?

Phil But who throws out a little packet of powder?

Pete I don't care.

Phil A terrorist who's seen the error of his ways, that's who.

Pete Listen Phil, there's no terrorist seeing the error of his ways, there's no Muslim men's club making poison in their back kitchen with a pot and a pan, there's no addict with two kids, and there's no Frank fucking Sinatra Junior eating beef and onion crisps in the park.

Phil And there's no God.

Pete There's no what?

Phil You were going to tell me there's no God.

Pete I was not.

Phil It just seemed like you was on a roll, is all.

Pete Well, you know what? There is no God, yeah? Not in this bin.

Phil Maybe not but . . .

Pete *(holding out the packet of powder)* You're not gonna find anything but a bunch of beauty products.

Phil OK, fine, but . . .

Pete Now please don't say that shit again.

Phil You do find the odd diamond, Pete.

Bus Stop

Play no. 52

(An art teacher speaks to his student in a girls' school in Berkshire)

Leo Or not. Or not. We could continue the tutorial here if you'd like.

Ann Why would I need to go to your house?

Leo No one needs to do anything. No one is saying you need to.

Ann You want me to.

Leo Only if you yourself want to. You know you're not being forced.

Ann To study at your house. What about your wife?

Leo It's just a tutorial.

Ann What about her, though?

Leo Well, why should that matter? I'm your teacher. I'm interested in your life. It's fine.

Ann She might find it a bit strange.

Leo Well, she's actually not living there any longer. OK? Not that that means . . . I'm just saying there are many ways to learn.

Ann Probably quickly is the way I'm looking for right now.

Leo Sometimes an informal atmosphere is more conducive.

Ann Why would going to your house be conclusive?

Leo No. Let's just say it would be better. Better. More comfortable for you. And you said you once wondered what my house must be like.

Ann Why would I say that?

Leo You wondered if it was as messy as my desk.

Ann I don't remember saying that at all.

Leo It must have been a joke. We have a laugh, don't we? You don't think of me as just your teacher.

Ann Yeah. You said we should all think of you as a friend.

Leo Exactly. So why don't you say that?

Ann We all think of you as a friend.

Leo Maybe you think of me as an important friend. Someone you want to make a connection with.

Ann I'm just a bit worried about my test scores, really.

Leo Art is about feeling. It's not always about what's in an art history textbook.

Ann Except the course is art history.

Leo It's also about making art, making discoveries, making connections.

Ann I've been memorising, like, all week.

Leo I know. But, you see, that's what is wrong with this system. You girls think you can just memorise, don't you? Just use me to help you memorise.

Ann Maybe we should finish the tutorial right here.

Leo You don't know how lucky you are to have this kind of instruction. You could be going to a comprehensive.

Play no. 53

(A bald man sits with two others in a gym steam room in Liverpool)

Ed These days – no lie – his are the size of two Maltesers.
Joe They shrunk down that much, did they?
Ed I tell a lie. They're more like two peanut M&Ms.
Dave What, were you looking at them in the shower or something?
Ed No. He told me, didn't he? Almost in tears, he was.
Joe Not bloody likely. Not like Willsy to be crying and all.
Ed Willsy says to me, he says, just warn the lads. It could happen to them.
Dave He always said he loved injecting.
Ed For a while. It's a good hobby for a lad for a short time.
Dave He said it was the best thing he ever done. Besides tanning.
Joe It could've been anything that shrunk him down.
Ed Yeah? Like what else?
Joe Like using a mobile.
Ed Using a mobile on his bollocks?
Joe Maybe the mobile was too close to them.
Ed It weren't his mobile.
Dave He was doing jabs of anabol, wasn't he?
Ed He had a whole routine. He'd go into the loo, put a needle in his behind. It's not right, lads.
Joe Sure.
(pause)

	But his arms were massive though.
Dave	They were well nice, those arms.
Ed	But did you ever see his legs, lads? Like sticks they were.
Dave	I don't think girls look so much at the legs, though.
Ed	Fine. You jab yourself with what you like.
Joe	How small were his bollocks, again?
Ed	Probably more like regular-sized M&Ms, now that I think about it.
Joe	He had nice arms, though.
Dave	They were well-cut arms. And tanned.
Ed	His bollocks were more like raisins now that I think about it.
Joe	I thought you said Maltesers.
Ed	I'm just remembering the conversation more.
Joe	You can't say Maltesers and then say raisins.
Dave	I could live with Maltesers for arms like that. Not raisins though.
Joe	No way mate. Not raisins.

Play no. 54

(A father and daughter sit beneath a CCTV camera in Henley-on-Thames)

Lara Is it on all the time?

David Yes, sweetheart.

Lara What about at night?

David Certainly. That's when it needs to be on. When we're at home.

Lara Dad, why does it never take a break?

David It doesn't need to take a break.

Lara What if it gets dirty from someone touching it?

David No one can reach it. OK? Are we done now, sweetie? It's best to just ignore it. We'll have to be getting you home soon.

Lara What if a bird feather got in front and it couldn't see?

David Lara, they'd clean it up.

Lara Who would clean it?

David I don't know. The people who are in charge of . . .

Lara Who is in charge of the cameras, though?

David They're professionals. Now, have we had enough of that? You're getting ice cream on your fingers.

Lara Is the camera still on right now?

David Yes, it's still on, Lara.

Lara What if they see what I'm doing?

David I'm sure they would like you.

Lara What if they don't?

David Well, as long as you're not doing anything bad like annoying your father on a Saturday . . .

(pause)

No. Sweetheart, I'm sorry.

Lara But I'm not doing anything bad.

David I know. Daddy was just joking.

Lara I don't want to sit here now.

David We can go sit over by the other bench.

Lara There's another camera on that building. I can see it.

David Then we can go home.

Lara Can one of them see us when we're at home?

David Of course not. Of course not. Don't be silly.

Lara Who is watching it, though?

David I think it's time for a nap. Listen, the more there are, the safer we are.

Lara From who?

David From . . . here, give me that ice cream. From people who don't . . .

Lara But it's looking at me still. It's looking at me.

David From people, all right? Now that's enough. I don't want to hear another word till we're home. That's enough.

Play no. 55

(A man approaches a woman at a small party in a pub near London Bridge)

Barry	Thanks for what you wrote on my leaving card.
Sarah	Oh. Did I forget to sign it?
Barry	No. I appreciated what you said.
Sarah	Well, you're welcome, Jerry.
Barry	It's actually Barry. Baz.
Sarah	Right, I'm sorry. That's embarrassing. Sorry.
Barry	What you said was close enough. Rhymes.
Sarah	But you're having a good leaving do? They get you a good prezzie?
Barry	Apparently you have to be here a year to get a present.
Sarah	Really? At least they bought you a pint.
Barry	I bought this one. But . . . *(pause)* Strange that this is the first time we've spoken face to face.
Sarah	You know how these offices can be. Now you're leaving . . .
Barry	I guess you don't remember my voice?
Sarah	Why? You on the radio, then?
Barry	No. Two and a half weeks ago? A problem with the mouse?
Sarah	The mouse in my kitchen?
Barry	No, attached to your computer. You called IT. You said to me 'Thanks very, very much' at the end of my consultation.

Sarah Did I?

Barry 'Very, very much.' Two 'very's.

Sarah Well, thanks again. Very much. It's working now.

Barry I was just surprised to see you showing such emotion with what you wrote on my card.

Sarah Oh. I'm glad you liked it.

Barry I think you were really speaking from the heart; probably saying what you'd always wanted to say.

Sarah It just showed up on my desk, really.

Barry I read it over a few times: keep in touch. That's what you wrote.

Sarah Did I? I'm sure everyone would appreciate an update from the new place. Where are you going again?

Barry I'm just going to take some time off.

Sarah To go travelling? See the world?

Barry I'm moving back in with my parents, just to regroup.

Sarah Lovely.

Barry No, I really don't get along with them. I hate them, actually. Any distraction would be good. Any reason to get back into the city.

Sarah Right.

Barry So how should we . . .?

Sarah Should we what?

Barry Keep in touch.

Sarah Oh, maybe just send an email to all of us.

Barry Do you want to tell me where you live?

Sarah I was really just saying keep in touch with us, the group, the company. You know?

Barry I can write down your address here on the back of the card. Or just your mobile.

Play no. 56

(A nurse sits in an elderly woman's house in Richmond)

Irene And now just tell me your job, again?

Marian Long-term care. I'm going to ask you a few questions.

Irene And have I offered you some tea?

Marian I've finished a cup already, Mrs Good. I'm going to ask you some questions about your hip.

Irene I haven't broken it again, have I?

Marian Not at all.

Irene It's been broken in the past.

Marian Now it's all healed, is that right?

Irene Was that thanks to you? You were at the hospital, weren't you?

Marian No, Mrs Good. My job is care in the community.

Irene That's lovely and we must get you some tea.

Marian I've just had this cupful.

Irene Yes. Those are lovely cups, aren't they? I should get some for my own house.

(pause)

Marian Well, my job is to make sure you can stay here, right here, in your own house.

Irene Thank you. You're a very kind-looking person. I certainly appreciate your offer.

Marian Now I'm just going to ask you a few simple things.

Irene Shouldn't I be the one making the enquiries?

Marian Do you have questions you'd like to ask instead?

Irene If you are going to be working in this house I'll need to know if you are honest.

Marian If I'm to be working here?

Irene And if you come with good references. I haven't had a girl working at the house in years.

Marian And where is your house?

Irene It's not far from here.

Marian And where are we right now?

Irene This hotel room simply won't do, will it? I can't even offer someone a cup of tea here. You don't like this room, do you?

Marian Why don't we talk about your fall.

Irene It was a simple mistake. It won't happen again.

Marian Could you point out where it happened?

Irene Just over there by the stairs.

Marian In this hotel room?

Irene Oh no, no, no. This is my home. The home I'm going to stay in. I don't fall often.

Marian Sorry, I thought you'd fallen only once.

Irene I want to stay in the house. Have I not been welcoming?

Marian You're very welcoming.

Irene I haven't even offered you some tea.
(pause)
What are you writing there?

Marian Just a few notes, Mrs Good.

Irene Now, you'll have to tell me what it is you do again.

Marian I'm in care in the community.

Irene That sounds fascinating. I thought for a moment you worked for the hotel.

Play no. 57

(Evening. Two women sit at desks opposite each other in an office in Manchester)

Eva	Did you carry on with the client last night?
Leonie	Of course. Till about 2am.
Eva	You two seemed to really have a connection.
Leonie	I believe in making that connection.
Eva	Oh, absolutely.
Leonie	No, but a serious connection. You were quite friendly with them.
Eva	I try to be welcoming.
Leonie	But I'm really looking into people's souls. Spending real time.
Eva	Oh, absolutely.
Leonie	I mean, I would love to just go home like some people. I would just love, absolutely love, to have a life.
Eva	You should take more time. I've noticed that.
Leonie	I would just love to. I wish I could.
Eva	You don't have to stay this late. No one does. Look how deserted the place is.
Leonie	I tell myself that. It's just . . .
Eva	Is everything all right?
Leonie	It's very hard. Hard when you care so much about the company. You know how it is. Every waking moment. I'm sure you know.

Eva Oh, absolutely.

(pause)

Well, I've got to pick my son up.

Leonie Of course. Sons and daughters – beautiful things. I'd love to have children some day.

Eva Really? I've never heard you . . .

Leonie Oh yeah, I think about it all the time. You're so lucky to have a reason to leave early.

Eva I don't leave that early.

Leonie And the rest of the team don't mind at all. It's not that your work suffers.

Eva Well, it doesn't suffer.

Leonie Absolutely. I completely agree. Completely. You just have a really good reason to push off. You'd better get going.

Eva Don't stay for too much longer. Please.

Leonie Don't worry about me. I envy you.

Eva What time do you think you'll finish?

Leonie Not much longer. An hour. Two at the most. I'm waiting to call the team leader in Los Angeles.

Eva Oh yes. She's quite a nice person.

Leonie We've made a connection. Deep. You know how it is when you care.

Play no. 58

(A woman speaks into a mobile in central London.)

A fireman. A sexy fireman. And she only put it in her mouth for, like, less than a second so it doesn't really count that much. Who knows what he did up in Edinburgh.
(pause)
Beautiful. It's in the country. Just really traditional. You know, like traditional stones and pews. I think they really believe in that.
(pause)
White fabric. And it's really beautiful. Really pure, you know?

Play no. 59

(A woman speaks to a young man near a playground in a park in Leicester)

Jill	But then, rain tomorrow, is what the forecast said.
Tim	All the more reason to enjoy the weather today.
Jill	They certainly do. Mine's the one over there screaming, naturally.
Tim	It's good to hear the sound of kids.
Jill	At seven girls learn how to scream in a whole new way, as you probably know.
Tim	No. None of them are mine.
Jill	Oh really? You're just in the park?
Tim	Seemed like a beautiful day.
Jill	Sure. This park wouldn't be my choice if I was a man all by myself, though. All the screaming and all.
Tim	I don't mind.
Jill	All the children running about. It's not really relaxing.
Tim	I like coming here.
Jill	You like looking at the kids?
Tim	I'm not really watching them.
Jill	Not really watching? Just sort of watching? I guess they're quite hard to miss.
Tim	Perhaps.
Jill	It's just we have an unofficial policy.

Tim I'm sorry. Who is we?

Jill The mothers and I – you can see a few of them round here. It's just good for us to talk to any man who shows up here.

Tim To the park?

Jill Because of all the . . . well, you know why. Blink of an eye and all.

Tim Sure. I wish you all the best. I should get back to my book.

Jill You're reading Nabokov?

Tim Yes. I didn't know that's how you pronounced it. It's just for a course is all.

Jill Are you a fan of him?

Tim I really don't know his work.

Jill He had some interesting things to say about children, or so I've heard.

Tim These are just some of his stories.

Jill Things to say about girls, or so I've heard.

Tim Well, it's been very nice to meet you.

Jill And you. It's a shame your bench is in the shade now. Not so great for reading.

Tim This is fine. I find it hard to read in the sunlight. I usually wear sunglasses.

Jill When you come to this park?

Tim Just on a sunny day in general.

Jill There are some benches over there that are quite nice and shaded. By the road.

Tim Thank you. I'll keep that in mind.

Jill I think you should. I really just think you should.

Play no. 60

(A mother and daughter walk to the back of a pub near Russell Square. White wine for the elder, a half pint of bitter for the younger. A television is broadcasting cricket in the corner)

Alexandra Mum, finish the story. Did he pick you up in a nice car?

Penelope Who? Your brother?

Alexandra No, last Friday night. I want details.

Penelope Oh, stop it.

Alexandra He picked you up in his nice car. He was wearing an interesting tie, Ru said. You have to tell me about the romance, Mummy.

Penelope This is not a mountain. This is a molehill.

Alexandra He took you to the Ivy.

Penelope No, to the Indian. Down at the end of the street.

Alexandra That's a bit cheap.

Penelope It was informal.

Alexandra With him in his tie?

Penelope Alexandra, I don't know. He was fine. A little different from what I had imagined. He seemed to be bewildered by the city. I've never heard someone talk so much about the ring road. The ring road this, the traffic, the feeder lanes, the amount of single passenger cars on the M25. I didn't know what to say. I thought all this talk of traffic meant he was trying to stay the night.

Alexandra With you? On the first date?

Penelope Not in our house.

Alexandra He could have used my room.

Penelope Not in your room, Alexandra. I told him that this was all new for me. I was nervous. I said I absolutely adored my children.

Alexandra Why?

Penelope Because I do.

Alexandra Why did that come up?

Penelope He told me his passion was the outdoors. He asked me if I had any passions.

Alexandra Your garden.

Penelope He said passions.

Alexandra You have passions that aren't your children, Mum. Don't say we're your passion.

Penelope It's the truth.

Alexandra It makes people nervous. Men.

Penelope You and Rupert are my life. I wanted him to know that whatever happened he would never be as important to me as you two.

Alexandra Perfect.

Penelope You know I love you.

Alexandra I know that.

Penelope We don't say it enough, do we?

Alexandra We say it.

Penelope I had to say something to put an end to all his talk of the outdoors and foxhunting. He knows those men who broke into the House of Commons to protest. I would have been there, he said, but they wanted young men who didn't have large stomachs. Yes, well. I just smiled at that. I didn't know what to say when he was talking about the smell of his saddle and how lovely it was. I suppose he meant the leather but I thought he was speaking about his own smell. Himself.

Alexandra Mum.

Penelope I wasn't sure if it was just his way of talking about, you know, his crotch. It was odd. I guess everyone's vegetable patch is different.

Alexandra He's handsome though, from what Rupert said.

Penelope More outdoorsy than handsome.

Alexandra Like Dad.

Penelope Your father was not outdoorsy.

Alexandra He was tanned.

Penelope He wasn't ruddy. I shouldn't be cruel. He said to me, 'My passion is foxhunting.' Although it's different for him, he said, because he truly understands the animal. He read some book on the American Indian and how it had a soul connection with its prey. So he has that too, apparently. He's very serious. Some people on the hunts are foolish, as you might expect.

Alexandra Daddy thought hunts were ridiculous.

Penelope He didn't act foolishly at them.

Alexandra He always said they were ridiculous.

Penelope Your father wasn't foolish.

(pause)

So, anyway, he said he could feel what the animal was feeling. I told him I could understand that.

Alexandra What a fox is feeling?

Penelope No, I said I found it hard not to feel what my children were feeling.

Alexandra Mum.

Penelope Do you remember at the old place in Finchley when you slipped and shoved your leg into the doorframe? You had just got out of the bath and you were running naked.

Alexandra You told him I was naked?

Penelope You had come straight from the bath.

Alexandra You don't talk about your daughter being naked.

Penelope Your knee was almost skinned to the bone. I almost couldn't stand to look at it. Your father put his arms around me and said that I was the one who was supposed to be calm. I was the one who was supposed to hold it together and he was right. We picked you up. You don't remember. The two of us linked arms underneath you and it calmed me. He could always calm me down. He would just hold on to me for minutes on end. And do you remember his voice?

Alexandra You didn't talk to him about Daddy's voice, did you?

Penelope It's not wrong to talk about your father. We don't do it enough. I won't be told how I should mourn. It's hardly been a year, or a couple of years.

Alexandra But on a date?

Penelope A dinner.

Alexandra Your first dinner. With anyone.

Penelope It was just dinner. I told him during the meal that I sometimes can't even remember the sound of your father's voice.

Alexandra When? During pudding?

Penelope We had decided not to have pudding.

Alexandra Who decided?

Penelope There didn't seem to be a point. Our meals were very filling.
(pause)

Alexandra, people have their own kinds of conversation when they reach this age. And he was interested. I told him sometimes I have to sit there in the quiet just to hear your father's voice. Some nights I have to lie in the dark and try to bring back just any small word. He knew your father. From school.

Alexandra I know.

Penelope He told me that once your father had to stand up and recite some William Blake. His voice had already deepened and all the boys were quite jealous. I told him I wished I could hear his voice right then.

Alexandra He must have enjoyed that.

Penelope It's all right to talk about these things. He had his own example.

Alexandra His ex-wife is not dead. She lives in Scotland.

Penelope Not her. He said on some days he couldn't remember the bark of one of his favourite hounds.

(pause)

Alexandra Mum.

Penelope I just looked down at my fork.

Alexandra He was making a joke.

Penelope He wasn't.

Alexandra Oh, Mum.

Penelope Then we had to drive back. We had to drive fifty feet down the street. He insisted. So that was another chance to complain about the cars. We stopped in front of the house. He couldn't park because of the traffic so he said it would have to be a quick goodbye.

Alexandra Did he kiss you?

Penelope Alexandra.

Alexandra Mum.

Penelope I don't know what it was. He came in towards me. I got that feeling that used to come at the end of our Christmas party when your father's friend would kiss me goodbye for too long. I felt unfaithful. His face was so large coming towards me. And the worst thing. This is terrible.

Alexandra It's all right.

Penelope I noticed there was something, some sort of chicken korma sauce on his moustache.

Alexandra Oh, Mum.

Play no. 61

(Two young Australians watch cricket in a pub in Leeds)

Baz Is that clear?

Ethan Yeah, I get it.

Baz I'm happy for them, too.

Ethan I was just celebrating that catch.

Baz You don't have to, you know, touch me every time there's a decent ball.

Ethan I didn't.

Baz You did. On the shoulder.

Ethan You're my oldest mate.

Baz All right.

Ethan The only one I really know here.

Baz For now.

Ethan It's just strange to be watching this from so far. Remember those spring rolls we used to eat when we watched the cricket?

Baz We only ate them once.

Ethan I used to, like, feed them to you when your arm was in that sling.

Baz You did that once.

Ethan I miss all that. A lot. It's so damp here. They keep making me put a bucket on the fruit machine at the pub to catch the leaks. Even the rain is disgusting.

Baz Watch the telly.

Ethan Sorry I touched you.
Baz Mate, I'm all for celebration.
Ethan I wanted to feel close.
Baz Yup. Fine. Come on, boys.
Ethan It feels nice to be close.
(pause)
It's just, when I see the cricket, I think of all the times we were in the sun, big-screen TV, eating those spring rolls.
Baz That's your hand on my shoulder.
Ethan Sorry.
Baz Seriously, mate, your hand is on my shoulder.
Ethan I just . . .
Baz I don't want it there.
Ethan I'm just happy with how well we're doing. And that catch, you know?

Play no. 62

(A man stands next to a woman in Canal Street in Manchester)

Jon OK, I don't need to be reminded.

Lyn You signed the agreement.

Jon Don't I know what I signed? It's my signature.

Lyn You knew about Susan long before.

Jon She was there when we met.

Lyn And it's not like we didn't pay you. You came out of it quite well.

Jon It was different then. You look really good now. All tanned. Your hair is longer.

Lyn Jon, I chose you because you said you hated marriage, hated the government and hated everything about this visa process. You wanted to help.

Jon I think you were more of a lesbian before.

Lyn What, before we got married?

Jon Do you remember our reception?

Lyn Yes. It's hard to forget kissing someone with a beard.

Jon You danced with Susan instead of me.

Lyn Of course I did. She's my partner.

Jon I was your husband. Am. Legally, if you need reminding.

Lyn When have we ever spent a single night together?

Jon When have you ever asked me to?

Lyn You're a beard, Jon.

Jon I shaved it off.

Lyn Are a beard, not have. You're a Home Office husband.

Jon You told my mother you wanted kids.

Lyn She's a terrifying woman with a cross around her neck.

Jon I guess those photos in Brighton mean nothing.

Lyn The ones we took as proof for the Home Office?

Jon You kissed me in them. More than once.

Lyn Do you know how gay I really am?

Jon You said vows that I wrote. On paper.

Lyn How else do you get a visa to this ridiculous country? It was just immigration, Jon.

Jon It's never just immigration.

Play no. 63

(Two women sit on a bus heading towards Lewisham)

Louise The last one was just better.

Annie Definitely better-looking.

Louise Even when he was all old and shaking all over the place you just wanted to sit him down and give him a biscuit.

Annie He had a cute little face.

Louise Kind of like a teddy bear, wasn't it?

Annie He was good-looking when he was young too, before he was the Pope.

Louise This new Pope was a Nazi.

Annie He wasn't a real Nazi.

Louise He was a young Nazi. I read that somewhere. And you know how you just don't get along with some people? I just don't like his face. You know who he looks like? Remember Ed from the mail room?

Annie With the red trainers?

Louise They have the same face.

Annie Him and the Pope?

Louise Same shape.

Annie I always fancied Ed a little.

Louise I saw Ed after that new Pope came in and for days I would be looking at his face when he came pushing his cart around. Finally, I just thought, that's the Pope. And that Ed was always putting his foot in it, too.

Annie He had a nice build, though.

Louise He told a joke one Thursday about the Paralympics. Worst thing I ever heard. He had to apologise. No one really looked at him the next day. He came and put the post on my desk and I didn't even look up.

Annie It's a bit different from having to apologise to the Muslim world.

Louise No one even looked at him all day.
(pause)
Did you really fancy Ed?

Annie If you had to pick from the mail room.

Louise Even with his jokes?

Annie I didn't know till now, did I?

Louise I couldn't go near Ed. It would be like snogging the Pope. Or a young Nazi.

Annie The Pope wasn't a Nazi.

Louise That's just what I read.
(pause)
Though I do sort of fancy that one from the Church of England.

Annie The one with the beard?

Louise Rowan Atkinson.

Annie It's not Rowan Atkinson.

Louise It's a Rowan. And he hardly ever has to apologise. That's a good sign.

Play no. 64

(Two sisters are on a train home to Suffolk)

Paula I had to send Sarah. I've told you about Sarah? My new PA, Sarah?

Juliet A few times.

Paula I had to send Sarah out in the lunch hour to get the gift. She thinks 'reasonable' means £400. For Mum.

Juliet I decided to donate to a charity in Mum's name.

Paula What, as a gift? Does that count?

Juliet Why wouldn't it?

Paula Mum says it's one of those things you do regardless. And she says it's nice to have something under the tree because, you know, a person can't exactly wear Darfur. But I guess a donation is better than more of your Fairtrade socks.

Juliet I know how you feel about the socks.

Paula I didn't even have to feel them.

Juliet They were very ethical.

Paula She's the one who got a rash from that llama fur.

Juliet No one gets rashes from alpaca. And this year she'll know I put fifty quid towards something in her name.

Paula Is it that Eastern European orphanage again?

Juliet In Albania.

Paula I'm doing Romania. Just a little home for handicapped orphans and, I think, blind children, too. In Mum's name. But she'll still have something under the tree. You should see the brooch Sarah picked out.

Juliet Mum prefers ethical presents.

Paula She always says she does, doesn't she?

Juliet Because she does.

Paula How is her Christmas goat from last year?

Juliet Mum liked the goat.

Paula It never writes.

Juliet She liked the goat.

(pause)

Paula Hard to wear one, though.

Play no. 65

(Two DJs prepare for a New Year's Eve party in Watford)

Andy Ange says I get midnight.

Sam No. I've got records for midnight. I get midnight.

Andy Yeah, mate, you actually got it last year.

Sam And I believe that was described as incredible.

Andy Ange is like, 'Things is different this year.'

Sam No way. I get the tone right. I know tone.

Andy I know tone, too.

Sam But I get the build. Right up to midnight, it's that build.

Andy I build.

Sam But I'm assembling, yeah? You're the apprentice. Last year? That was the work of a craftsman. Midnight, the set climaxes, everyone does the countdown and then, boom. It was an explosion. It ripped the place apart. It was violence.

Andy I don't know if she wants that.

Sam You never heard sound like that before. Like, blam. Why aren't we in that same room this year?

Andy It don't have wheelchair access.

Sam So what?

Andy Ange needs wheelchair access.

Sam Since when?

Andy For her boyfriend . . .

Sam What, that massive bloke?

Andy Yeah.

Sam The skinhead guy?

Andy It's a shaved head. They shave it in the military.

Sam He wasn't in a wheelchair last year.

(pause)

Oh, yeah.

Andy Yeah.

Sam But then, don't the doctors give them, like, fake legs?

Andy Eventually.

Sam I mean, no disrespect to what he done in . . . where?

Andy He was over there, wasn't he?

Sam But it's like, you put a wheelchair out on the floor and it's hard to get everyone dancing.

Andy I think I should do midnight.

Sam It's hard for us to properly party.

Play no. 66

(A brother and sister stand on a train platform in Egham, Surrey)

Leo Get away from me. You've got nothing to trade.

Mia I've got clips on my phone.

Leo Yeah, probably SpongeBob.

Mia I've got Christina Aguilera.

Leo Wearing what?

Mia A dress.

Leo Maybe if she was naked.

Mia Stop being such a dick.

Leo Then stop being a dick in a box.

Mia I'll tell Mum you've got Saddam on your phone.

Leo I'd just erase it.

Mia I'd still tell her.

Leo So what? It would be gone.

Mia It'd be like when she found out about those websites you went to . . . Just let me see it. You showed Carl.

Leo I traded him 'cos he had a good clip.

Mia Of what?

Leo Of a black kid punching some guy on the Metropolitan Line. Besides, you can't handle seeing someone hanging.

Mia I can so.

Leo You don't even know what a dead person looks like.

Mia Grandad.

Leo He wasn't dead when you saw him.

Mia He was ill.

Leo He wasn't hanging in some Iraqi jail getting yelled at. You see everything on this clip.

Mia Why d'you want to see everything?

Leo Because it's important.

Mia Why?

Leo Because it's, like, history.

Mia It's sick.

Leo Yeah, well, history is sick. Like the Nazis and the . . . Romans.

Mia That's not history, that's *Gladiator*. You're just sick.

Leo Then go watch SpongeBob.

Mia I'll see it on Julie's phone.

Leo Like your friends would have it.

(pause)

Mia Leo?

Leo And I'm not trading for any of your stupid MP3s.

Mia Can I just see the beginning? Just the start?

Play no. 67

(A man walks into a sexual health clinic in Norwich)

Richard Peter?
(pause)
Peter?

Peter Oh. Hello.

Richard It's Richard.

Peter Yes. I know.

Richard Mind if I sit with you? Not the most likely place to see you, is it? You're well?

Peter Of course I am.

Richard I mean you're doing well?

Peter Yes. It's just a check-up.

Richard Good, good. I'm just here for a check-up as well. It's been ages, you devil. I saw the photos from your wedding. Beautiful day for you and Suzanne. You remember it rained on ours.

Peter I remember.

Richard I didn't get the invite to yours. I guess it was an intimate ceremony. You got our gift? The salad bowl.

Peter We use it.

Richard Give it an old toss.

Peter We use it occasionally.
(pause)

Richard This is a hard place to find. I suppose it's your first time, too.

Peter Yes.

Richard I had to ask directions. Where's the old sex clinic, I said. And then you run into someone you've known for ages. So strange.

Peter I suppose your wife will be picking you up.

Richard No. Yours?

Peter No.

(pause)

Richard It's taking some time, isn't it? Doesn't usually take this long.

Peter I wouldn't know.

Richard Me neither. Well. If you're going to be telling your wife you saw me today, please give her my regards.

Peter If you're going to be telling your wife you saw me today, give her my regards as well.

Play no. 68

(At a pub in Colburn, two parents sip halves of lager)

Dave	The server.
Maureen	What's the server?
Dave	The thing, the computer thing, that sends out the emails.
Maureen	You'd expect the British Army to have a good serving.
Dave	It's a server, Maureen. Sometimes it just doesn't work for a while, especially in that part of the world. *(pause)*
Maureen	He'll write.
Dave	There's nothing wrong. He'll write.

THEATRE

Play no. 69

(Two older chauffeurs wait at Arrivals at Heathrow. They hold signs bearing names)

Alf — I've always admired your 'i's. I never did have strong 'i's.

Pat — I've only got one 'i'. In this name.

Alf — It's the way you dot them, though, isn't it?

Pat — I sometimes do stars for the men. Hearts for the ladies. It's that personal touch.

Alf — Are they paying more for that?

Pat — All free of charge, mate. You see these younger blokes using a computer to make theirs. No. I'm a hand-writer.

Alf — I've always been a hand-writer. That's why I stand next to you.
(pause)
I used to have a few flourishes. Back in the day.

Pat — Mate, you have no idea.

Alf — I do. I was known for my accents before the Chunnel was built. My French accents were razor sharp.

Pat — Back then I'd have the hugest letters on all my signs. I didn't even care when I was starting out.

Alf — It used to be a free-for-all, didn't it?

Pat — Used to be a true expression.

Alf — I wrote one name in mauve when I was going through my mauve phase.

Pat — And do you remember your first Japanese characters?

Alf	I had the steadiest hands back then.
Pat	Who are you picking up these days?
Alf	Oh, I do these Russians now. All them rich ones.
Pat	I stay away from that sort. Such long names.
Alf	I've had to start using a smaller pen.
Pat	Never get a smaller pen. You might as well retire.
Alf	My wife says, 'You're going to ruin your wrist doing it that small.'
Pat	They're grunters, those Russians.
Alf	Never say a word.
Pat	They look at you with cold eyes.
Alf	Sometimes I'll write out a long name and think, 'Who are you? Are you going to ask me my name?' They never do.
Pat	You do a lovely 'e' though, mate. I always liked your 'e'. Never lose sight of that.

Play no. 70

(One couple watches another couple quickly exit a bar in Bootle)

Tez She'll be all right. You see what I was saying about his temper, though? It's hilarious.

Jo You should go after them.

Tez You think I chase after him every time he gives her a little tap? You'll get to know him. He's just like that.

Jo Just like that when he shoves her, is he?

Tez He didn't touch her face.

Jo Near enough her face.

Tez It doesn't count if it's not the face, that's what he says.
(pause)
When he's joking. That's that sense of humour.

Jo Hilarious.

Tez He did say he liked you.

Jo Oh, did he, now?

Tez He said he hoped you weren't a foreigner with that last name of yours. But he's just having a laugh.

Jo And he's your best mate?

Tez Well, he's a mate, yeah.

Jo You said your best mate in the world.

Tez You're not going to make him politically correct, I'll tell you that. He says that's all gone mad, anyway, that PC. Shall we have another?

Jo All she said to him was one thing about Liverpool's keeper.

Tez You don't go nit-picking someone's club. No one does that to me.

Jo Or your mate. Your best mate.

Tez They have great nights out, those two. That night we won the Champions' League, they were on good form. When we won the FA Cup, he sang outside her window.

Jo So she wasn't exactly out with you?

Tez She was after he woke her. Catch him after a win and he's a great bloke.

Jo She was embarrassed to be here.

Tez That's her, isn't it?

Jo And nearly in tears in front of me.

Tez If she could have it her way, she'd be in tears most of the time. You're not like that.
(pause)
I said you're not like that.

Jo I think we should leave.

Tez You want another, don't you? One more?

Play no. 71

(Two men sit in a restaurant in Old Compton Street, London)

Ed So finally I thought, I am what I am. I can't lie any more. Luckily, my divorce was fairly perfect.

Joe Oh? You don't hear that too often.

Ed It was amicable. For me.

Joe I've never been contacted by a man with children.

Ed Toddlers. It's hard, but there are helpful children's books these days to explain it – *Daddy's Got a Boyfriend.*

Joe I'm not interested in becoming anyone's daddy. Or anyone's boyfriend.

Ed Of course not. This is just a date.

Joe I don't call them dates.

Ed Fine. Then whatever you call them in London.

Joe Is there not much of a gay scene back in Guildford?

Ed No. I'm ready for freedom now. I would never have bought a shirt like this in Guildford, would I?

Joe It's very shiny.

Ed I'm ready to dive into the whole scene.

Joe At least the whole scene isn't tired of you.

Ed Are you well known around here?
(pause)

Joe Yes.

Ed I liked your ad. It was simple. There are so many codes in gay life. I thought CD meant compact disc.

Joe	I'm not a cross-dresser.

Ed	I know. I liked what you said. I remember the first time I water-skied. I didn't know when to let go.

Joe	I've never been water-skiing.

Ed	So you're more into kayaking?

Joe	I don't like the outdoors.

Ed	So scuba diving in a pool?

Joe	What are you going on about?

Ed	You mentioned water sports.

Joe	It's a different kind of water sport.

Ed	Perhaps it's . . . not something I've heard of.

Joe	Perhaps it's better back in Guildford.

Play no. 72

(Two women stand at a lottery booth in a shopping precinct in Grimsby)

Viv You finally got winning numbers for us?

Pat I give you nice numbers every time.

Viv They're not winning at all so far.

Pat Should be keeping them for myself, then, shouldn't I?

Viv How much'll be going into my pocket this time?

Pat Listen to the peacock, preening before she's even won. It's only 3.2 this week, love.

Viv I'll take it with a smile.

Pat I wouldn't turn down 3.2, I'll tell you that much.

Viv I'd spend all her inheritance.

Pat How's the visit been then? Is Jenny driving back down tomorrow?

Viv Went today, didn't she, because they say they can't revise in a house what's always got the TV on.

Pat Couple of students. She didn't really say that.

Viv To be fair, it was her boyfriend who said that one.

Pat Because I was about to say it sounds like the boyfriend – the mouth on him.

Viv He gives me a lift here and says the lottery, it's just a tax on the stupid.

Pat Then he's calling you stupid to your face.

Viv To be fair, I don't play every week.

Pat I do.

(pause)

What a terrible thing to say. I got close the other week, didn't I?

Viv Which week?

Pat The other week. And I've just seen someone leave here with £35 today. That's not stupid.

Viv He says it's just the poor paying tax.

Pat It's how to become not-poor.

Viv She likes his theories. She hardly speaks to me all weekend.

Pat The mouth on him . . . You want me to pick your numbers, then?

Viv I don't know, really. Think I'll have a lucky dip instead.

Play no. 73

(Two teenagers drink alcopops in a park in Portsmouth)

Toby The bra is off by then, yeah?

Rhys No, just snogging. Or just before the beginning of snogging.

Toby When you're leaning in?

Rhys Yeah, like, tilting my head.

Toby Which way do you tilt?

Rhys Uh, to the right.

Toby Me, too. I totally tilt to the right.

Rhys Then the tears start. I say to her, 'What are you thinking right now?'

Toby Never say, 'What are you thinking?'

Rhys I ask her, 'Did I do something wrong?'

Toby After 'What are you thinking?' Those are the two worst things.

Rhys I had closed the curtains. There was, like, romantic music. Classical and shit.

Toby One of your soundtracks, wasn't it?

Rhys It's still classical.

Toby *Lord of the Rings*, wasn't it?

Rhys But all the slow tracks. Not, like, battle scenes.

Toby And you wonder why she started crying.

Rhys No, she says, 'I'm sorry. I can't. It's just I'm really worried about all that climate change.'

Toby What, is that a way of saying you have bad breath?

Rhys No, it's just all those polar bears.

Toby Those ones sinking through icebergs?

Rhys Into the water. And drowning.

Toby At two in the morning she's saying this?

Rhys Apparently there aren't going to be any more polar bears.

Toby Yeah, but polar bears aren't going to shag her. You said that, right?

Rhys No, I said I'd stop driving my car.

Toby For polar bears?

Rhys For her.

Toby And then at least you snogged her.

Rhys Well, she's sort of worried about the rainforest as well.

Play no. 74

(A young employee leans against the checkout of a supermarket on Holloway Road, north London)

AJ I've got my Honda here today. So nice. Didn't buy it used, neither.

Tina Don't like cars, do I?

AJ I got the mad flash rims.

Tina That's part of the car, yeah? Rims is still part of the car.

AJ I just want to please you.

Tina Whatever.

AJ I want to buy you flowers with colours like purple and make you eat chocolates you never tasted before.

Tina Why you even up here on your break?

AJ I just want to be with you, know what I'm saying? I want to be so close to you, I want to, like, be your nametag.

Tina You already had a fag?

AJ Yeah, but so quick I was choking so I could be with you. How much you love me?

Tina I'm on the Express till. I can't just be saying that. It's busy.

AJ How much?

Tina What about all them other things you said you'd nick for me?

AJ I got you CDs already.

Tina Don't like them ones.

AJ I got you Mariah Carey.

Tina You were all, like, I can nick you nice deli food. Like loads of meat.

AJ I could get you so much turkey. We can't sell none of that turkey now.

Tina Don't like turkey.

AJ I'm gonna slice it so thin.

Tina It kills you, don't it?

AJ You wouldn't even know it were turkey.

Tina You trying to kill me?

AJ No, I want to make you feel so nice. So nice, you know what I'm saying?

Tina You're trying to give me bird flu is what you're doing. I already had that ear infection this year.

AJ This is the truth, yeah? I'd never let a bird close to you what had bird flu. If I saw a turkey with that bird flu, I would throw it across the room.

Tina Whatever.

AJ That's what love is. That's what it is.

Play no. 75

(A man sits quietly across from his wife at a restaurant in Whitstable)

Susan	I'm just saying you never used to like oysters.
Nigel	I've always liked a good oyster.
Susan	You didn't on our honeymoon.
Nigel	I don't remember that.
Susan	What, the entire honeymoon?
Nigel	No, eating oysters.
Susan	You even refused them at my brother's wedding.
Nigel	Well, I'm dipping into them again.
Susan	You haven't been dipping with me.
Nigel	We haven't visited the seaside in a while, have we?
Susan	So who do you eat them with?
Nigel	For God's sake, Susan, this is supposed to be romantic.
Susan	It's just a question. They're not a food you eat with another man.
Nigel	Of course I can eat oysters with another man.
Susan	I wasn't born yesterday. I'm just curious as to who you'd be licking oysters with.
Nigel	Licking? So this is how it is? Even on holiday.
Susan	I'm just talking about oysters.
Nigel	I don't know how many times, and in how many ways, I've apologised. Repeatedly. It happened. It's over and I said I am sorry.

Susan You're saying she liked oysters.

Nigel No, I'm bloody well not.

Susan You've probably been here before. Do the staff recognise you?

Nigel I've never been here in my life.

Susan Of course. Sorry. All the receipts were from Cornwall.

(pause)

Nigel Have you phoned the children?

Susan No.

Nigel Well. It's nice to get away like this. Shall we share a plate of oysters?

Susan I won't touch them.

Nigel Then I might have a half dozen.

Susan I'd rather you had the fish pie.

Nigel They're all over the menu. It's one of the reasons I wanted to bloody come here. They're renowned.

Susan As aphrodisiacs. I think the fish pie looks just fine. With mayonnaise.

Play no. 76

(A man kisses a bride in a stairwell in Norwich)

Sue	Seriously, this has got to be the last time. Swear it.
Sam	You think I don't know that? He's my best mate.
Sue	Well, he's my husband now.
Sam	Our weekend in Blackpool was supposed to be the last time.
Sue	No, the last time officially was that one in your car.
Sam	When you were in the front?
Sue	With me in the back. You don't even remember.
Sam	That was the third to last time.
Sue	This ends. It ends. And don't make a mess. His sister did my make-up and the lashes are brand new. I have to, you know, get back in there.
Sam	To all the champagne.
Sue	I'm singing Abba with my bridesmaids.
Sam	How can I be quick if this is the last time? It's got to be memorable.
Sue	Don't kiss me full on the mouth.
Sam	Fine. I just wanted to say I've really enjoyed, you know, you.
Sue	What, is that supposed to be a sweet thing?
Sam	It's going to be hard to give this up. You up.
Sue	It's never been right.
Sam	Sometimes you've said quite loudly how right it is.
Sue	They're going to start singing soon. Quick.

Sam Maybe I don't want it to end like this.

Sue Then why did we come out here?

Sam Maybe I'll quit things on my own. Like having sex with you. And smoking.

Sue You think you can quit me and smoking? At once?

Sam If it's already taken away from me, what choice do I have? You're both, you know, unfeasible now.

Sue Don't call me unfeasible.

Sam Then don't . . . Don't say this is the last time. We could go outside. Far away from people. We could have one last one. A real official one.

(pause)

Sue I think I hear the Abba playing.

Play no. 77

(An elderly man queues with an American in a hotel in London)

Lionel I do apologise. So you're actually staying here?

Jim Oh yep.

Lionel Really? And you're paying?

Jim According to my credit card.

Lionel If you're guests, then please disregard what I said about my shoes. I wouldn't expect you to clean them.

Jim Yeah. You've got to talk to someone at the desk about that.

Lionel Lovely. And which part of Africa?

Jim I'm sorry? I'm not catching what you're saying. Your accent.

Lionel You're not from Tanganyika, are you?

Jim No, we're all from Philadelphia.

Lionel You see, my wife's eldest brother was posted to Tanganyika and had the most wonderful experience. Of course, we don't have colonies now. We're quite worthless.

Jim Not to us. You're important. You're with us.

Lionel We certainly had the discipline to run Tanganyika well.

Jim Well, it's all running well here.

Lionel My wife's brother even had a special cane, you see. He brought it back with him. So I hope you're not one of those ones who's running the place into the ground.

Jim Philly's got its problems, but we're trying our best.

Lionel You hear such terrible things from over there, don't you?

Jim Sure, but we've got some excellent sports teams.

Lionel We worked bloody hard. There was stability when we were there. My brother-in-law used to say, 'You can trust a white face.'

Jim Is that an English expression? Is that English?

Lionel Well, it's been a pleasure speaking with you. I wish I knew how to say goodbye in your language.

Jim It's just 'goodbye'.

Lionel That's very good. Well said. You've learned, haven't you?

Play no. 78

(Two women sit in a salon in Lancaster)

Helen	At least he doesn't sound like a freak.
Erica	God, Alan is so refreshingly normal.
Helen	Your last one read Japanese comic books, didn't he?
Erica	And he had dolls from sci-fi films. No, Alan's a real bloke. Big arms, nice tattoo.
Helen	And does he read?
Erica	Constantly. He read that new book about Diana in about a day and a half. And he read that one by Diana's butler and one about the paparazzi. He's always buying books.
Helen	What about his dating history?
Erica	Bit of a car wreck, he says. I don't mind that he hasn't been out with many.
Helen	Any long-term?
Erica	Not since '97. That's when things changed for him. But he wants me to be his princess.
Helen	He didn't say it like that!
Erica	All the time. It's so sweet. He bought me a tiara, as a joke.
Helen	That he makes you wear in bed?
Erica	As a joke.
Helen	In bed?
Erica	Once. It's just a little thing. I took it off eventually.
	(pause)

Helen The first night he stayed at yours?

Erica It was so lovely. So normal. I brought him coffee in the morning. He said it was the best he'd had since . . .

Helen Not his last girlfriend?

Erica No, since Diana died. He camped out in Kensington Gardens – all the rich people brought out coffee for them. It was the best he'd tasted. Until mine. I treat him like royalty.

Helen So why hasn't he got you over to his place yet?

Erica I'm staying tonight. He was joking today, said he'd have to get ready and take down all his photos.

Helen Well. He sounds unique.
(pause)
And you're happy.

Erica It's just normal, you know? I needed that.

Play no. 79

(Two men, slightly winded, stand at the peak of Snowdon in Wales)

Ollie He says unlike some people he doesn't have hair to keep him warm.

Chris It's summer. I didn't know it would be cold.

Ollie He wants your hat.

Chris Fine. Who forgot to bring his?

Ollie He says the one I brought makes him look like a cancer patient.

Chris He is a cancer patient.

Ollie He says this trip doesn't count without the view.

Chris Count? I can't control the mist. He asked for Snowdon. Here we are.

Ollie The whole point was the view.

Chris Do you know how hard it was to get permission from the hospital?

Ollie I pushed the wheelchair. I know.

Chris And to walk him here? Over rock?

Ollie He wants another wish. He wants an Arsenal game, too.

Chris No bleeding way. They all get one wish. That's how it works.

Ollie He thought the other nurse said one wish per month.

Chris No. It's one wish per illness. His was Snowdon. I have it written down.

Ollie To see the view for one last time.

Chris And this is the view. It's white. It's mist.

Ollie Maybe you didn't take into account global warming and the irregularity of the British summer.

Chris I'm a nurse, yeah? This is extracurricular.

Ollie It doesn't have to be Arsenal. We could take him bowling.

Chris I'd have to throw his ball and he wouldn't like the colour of the pins.

Ollie We could give him one more wish.

Chris Then they'll all be asking for one more. The whole ward.

Ollie It's their final wish.

Chris It's my weekend. Do you think I want to be in Wales?
(pause)

Ollie He also said there was supposed to be a café at the top.

Chris It's not finished yet. That's where all the drilling's coming from.

Ollie Well. He actually wanted a cappuccino, too.

Play no. 80

(It's late. A teenager holds a knife towards a man in Croydon)

Jay No, what did you say just then?
Theo I can take out cash. Loads.
Jay No, before that. When you was all acting tough.
Theo We can do this quietly and safely. Quickly. But safely.
Jay You called me a yob, didn't you?
Theo I did not. I mean yes, I did, but I say things I don't mean.
Jay You think I'm a yob? Look at these trousers.
Theo Your trousers? Right now?
Jay Look at them in the light.
Theo They're very sensible. Unless you want another pair. Is that what you . . .?
Jay I ain't got my trousers hanging down. You can't see my pants. See?
Theo They fit. Definitely.
Jay So I ain't no yob.
Theo No, of course not. It's just . . .
Jay What, you think I'm not wearing a belt? I am. Touch this belt.
Theo It is definitely a belt. It's a belt.
Jay So why you be calling me that?
Theo I'm sure I'm wrong, but yob . . .
Jay Don't keep saying it out loud, man.
Theo Sorry. That word doesn't refer to trousers.

Jay It stings, yeah? That word hurts me to, like, the bone of my existence.

Theo I don't want to hurt you. Maybe you don't want to hurt me.

Jay Every morning I have a fresh pair, yeah? Ironed, yeah? Who do you think does that?

Theo I'm sure you iron them brilliantly.

Jay I don't freaking iron my own trousers. But they're ironed, that's what I'm saying. What do you think that 'y' word means? That I'm stupid and can't read and I'm all dangerous?

Theo No, none of those things, clearly.

Jay Tell me what it means.

Theo Yob means people who don't wear trousers properly.

Jay And that's not me.

Theo Of course not. You have amazing . . . trousers.

Jay Right. Thank you. Now give me your pin number. Now.

Play no. 81

(A woman joins a man in the smoking area outside a hospital in Poole, Dorset)

Luke You've seen me in the gift shop.

Deb I thought we might have gone to uni together.

Luke No, the gift shop. It's an OK place to work. Lots of tat. And flowers.

Deb We've got so many flowers dying in the room upstairs.

Luke Is it your room?

Deb No, it's my boyfriend's room.

Luke Oh yeah. I thought you might have a boyfriend.

Deb They're beautiful for a while. I just can't stand the sight of a dying flower.

Luke Yeah. How sick is he, anyway?

Deb He hasn't regained consciousness.

Luke God, that must be terrible.

Deb He could wake up tomorrow. But people have stayed unconscious years.

Luke Even longer. It's a tragedy. And their girlfriends just sort of age.

Deb I've spent so much time in this hospital already.

Luke I know – you're in here every morning at eight.

Deb I read to him, you know?

Luke And I guess you were planning on being together a long time.

Deb Just started going out, really.

Luke But you were probably thinking of the future. Of eternity.

Deb I don't think of life that way. It's my duty to be here. Everyone says it is.

Luke I see lots of wives. They buy mints from me – usually Mentos. Of course, you're not his wife.

Deb His family don't give him support.

Luke But you're not his wife. Officially.

Deb I can't think straight. I've been wearing this same T-shirt for a week.

Luke I know. It's basically gone transparent.

(pause)

Deb I should get back upstairs.

Luke He'll still be there. Do you want some fags I stole from the shop?

Deb I'm smoking far too much.

Luke We could set up some sort of deal where I gave you a discount.

Deb I just turn to it in times of stress.

Luke Say thirty per cent off? Fifty if things get worse for him. If you need support.

Play no. 82

(A shopkeeper speaks to a man in Cheam)

Bob And your missus said you weren't directing the nativity this Christmas.

Tom No. That's not possible.

Bob Such a shame. With your new beard, you could play one of the wise men.

Tom I haven't been a very wise man recently.

Bob We don't see you with her in church these days.

Tom I've been taking time off.

Bob But people still say, 'I wonder if he'll do the nativity or even sing another duet with his missus at the service.'

Tom No duets.

Bob It was lovely. Your missus was in here the other day and that woman can talk, can't she, all chatting about your trip at New Year.

Tom I'm not exactly going.

Bob She said she was looking forward to it.

Tom She is.

(pause)

Bob OK. Is it just all these crisps today? You won't be ruining your tea, will you?

Tom That's not likely.

Bob And anything else?

Tom Cigarettes.

Bob OK . . . Which kind?

Tom Which do you recommend?

Bob Which do you smoke?

Tom I'm giving them all a go. And also some vodka.

Bob We've got some nice wine . . .

Tom I'll have the Russian bottle. Not the expensive one. The big bottle.

Bob Is that all?

Tom Maybe one more.

Bob Another bottle of vodka?

Tom Same size. Or one larger.

(pause)

Bob It looks like we'll just get one of the younger women to do the nativity this year.

Tom I'm sure you'll all be just fine.

Bob We feel it's important to get someone from the church.

Tom It is indeed.

Bob Thirty-six pounds thirty. Please.

Play no. 83

(Two homeless men sit in a Christmas shelter in east London)

Jake You think that's bad? One of them here told me that Jesus loves me no matter how I smell.

Liam And how were you smelling last Christmas then?

Jake Not bad: I had a wash before going to the shelter. Hair combed, the lot.

Liam One volunteer says to me last year, 'Can you believe the parking around here?'

Jake It's horrible, the suffering here.

Liam And another couldn't get a PlayStation at Woolworths.

Jake How do we sleep at night, Liam?

Liam Have you actually been sleeping?

Jake I meant in the looser sense.

Liam They've got all the old volunteers back. Like her over there . . .

Jake She still looks like John Major.

Liam She rubs your arm and says, 'It's OK. You're still worth something.'

Jake I thought she'd never stop.

Liam I thought she was going to set my arm on fire.

Jake She was having troubles last year, remember?

Liam Her family were refusing to speak to each other.

Jake You gave her some advice.

Liam For free. I volunteered it, really.

Jake It's hard seeing people with such problems at Christmas.

Liam Heard from your kids this year?

Jake I nearly did. I just reckon they're waiting to call me on New Year's Eve.

Liam Cheaper rates at New Year.

Jake Is that right?

Liam Don't know – could be.

Jake I'm sure they're just waiting for a bit of news big enough to tell me.

Liam That's got to be it.

Jake When was the last Christmas you heard from someone?

Liam Well, speaking of John Major . . .

Jake Sounds about right for me, too.
(pause)

Liam At least we don't have the problems of this lot.

Jake Apparently the parking round here is horrid, isn't it?

Play no. 84

(Two men stand in the small prayer room of an office in London)

Ali It's just I've never found the door locked before.

Alan I'm so sorry. I don't even remember locking it.

Ali You don't need to be sorry. It's a multi-faith room. All are welcome.

Alan I'll be done very soon.

Ali Shall I come back?

Alan I'm so sorry. I thought you only used it at certain times, that there were certain prayer times with you . . . You're Muslim, right?

Ali Yes. And may I ask . . .?

Alan I'm just like everyone else, praying to Jesus. I've seen your Qur'an and I'm respectful. I don't touch it.

Ali You're welcome to read it.

Alan God, no. Sorry. I just mean, I bring my own Book.

Ali Sure. OK.

Alan And that's a photo of Mecca there on the wall, right?

Ali Yes. I hope you're comfortable enough in the room.

Alan Pretty much, yeah. I think I've seen you around the office, by the way. Are you one of the IT guys?

Ali No.

Alan Are you sure? You really look like one of the IT guys.

Ali I work on the 11th floor.

Alan Oh, really? I'm on the eighth. Only the eighth. But I guess we're all equal in this room.

Ali Yes. There's just one thing. Do you mind not wearing shoes on our rug?

Alan What do you mean?

Ali You're standing on our rug.

Alan I thought it was just 'the' rug in the room.

Ali It's just a small request.

Play no. 85

(At a festival in Somerset, a young man and woman sit in a tent)

Terry Of course, that's totally acceptable.

Amy Because it is kind of a music festival, after all.

Terry It should be all about the music. You're right.

Amy It's just that I know people who have done things they've regretted at festivals.

Terry Like having sex with someone.

Amy Someone they knew only a little.

Terry But I guess in some cases that's part of the festival experience.

Amy I don't think it is, actually.

Terry For some people, I mean. Like, bad people.

Amy And there's no reason you couldn't just visit me in Grimsby after.

Terry Yeah. I hadn't thought of that.

Amy We could get to know each other.

Terry Sure. I'd be interested in doing that. In Grimsby.

Amy So it's not just like one night in a muddy tent.

Terry OK. Though a muddy tent thing can be quite good. For some people.

Amy And it's the last night as well.

Terry I know. But we've known each other for a lot longer than one day.

Amy A day and a half.

Terry	So you're saying you're not into getting to know each other in a festival sort of way?
Amy	No. Are you?
Terry	Of course not. No. It's just such a tradition, is all.
Amy	With you?
Terry	No, like historically. Festivals. Free love. Take a pill, see what happens. See what happens in the tent.
Amy	I just want it to be about the music.
Terry	That's exactly what I want, too. And maybe pills.
Amy	I guess I should have told you how I feel about drugs before. Just the idea of swallowing something . . .
Terry	I totally understand. Totally. *(pause)* Though you can crush them, you know. I mean, I'm just saying.

Play no. 86

(Two women stand in the late-night cold outside a club in Louth)

Lisa She was so minging tonight.

Kelly Well minging.

Lisa And that muffin top over her belt?

Kelly Does she not look at herself before she goes out? Does she not see the big roll of flubadub hanging over her belt? It's, like, cover it up.

Lisa It's, like, don't wear the halter-top, love.

Kelly And be happy whaling's banned.

Lisa It's not in Iceland.

Kelly Then be happy you're not there.

Lisa She was well minging.

Kelly She's, like, one further than munter.

Lisa Just basically munt.

Kelly And she's all on about the ASBO. Her ASBO. 'Oh, my ASBO.'

Lisa It's 'cos it's new.

Kelly So it's the best ASBO ever is it? I wanted to say to her: no one cares if you've got one now, munter. Last year, yeah. This year, no one cares.

Lisa All of Skegness has an ASBO now. Everybody who lives there.

Kelly Not everybody.

Lisa My cousin said if you leave your house you get one. Some guy got one for playing Coldplay too loud.

Kelly That's probably how she got hers. It's wasted on her. It just means the other ones aren't worth as much.

Lisa Remember Terry's?

Kelly See, Terry had a brilliant one.

Lisa He did something for it.

Kelly What's hers for, anyway? Munting?

Lisa Munting without a licence. Remember tonight, when she comes back with drinks and says, 'Oh, I had to use my elbows at the bar'?

Kelly Like she's suddenly ASBO hard.

Lisa When she really just pushed people out of the way with her muffin top.

Kelly I wouldn't even get an ASBO now. Not after her.

Lisa Me neither.

Kelly She just loves it too much.

Lisa She's an ASBO lover.

Kelly She's like an Asbian.

(pause)

Lisa Except then Terry pulled her.

Kelly He did not; he's driving her home.

Lisa That's not how it looked.

Kelly He's coming back for us.

Lisa OK.

Kelly He'll be back for us.

Play no. 87

(Two men sit next to each other in an open-plan office in Sunderland)

Phil See your cough's not actually gone.

Carl It was when I got up this morning.

Phil Still a bit phlegmy though, isn't it?

Carl I know it's on its way out.

Phil Sure, sure. Just not if you cough every two and a half minutes.

Carl I think that's an exaggeration.

Phil I've been timing it on this little clock on my computer.

Carl Well, calling it 'phlegmy' is an exaggeration.

Phil Even though I can still hear it all rattling about?

Carl That's not phlegm. That's the sound any lung makes.

Phil That wet and terrible sound?

Carl It's just what lungs are like.

Phil Does it sound so goopy when other people cough round here?

Carl Fine. Then I'll just stop then.

(pause)

(He coughs)

Phil It would be different if you could see them, though, wouldn't it?

Carl If I could see what?

Phil All the little invisible germs that are making their way over to me.

Carl I put my hand in front of my mouth, don't I?

Phil But I can almost see them curving around your hand.

Carl I don't agree.

Phil Just curling around and descending upon me.

Carl I'm not infectious.

Phil Just take another sick day, mate.

Carl I'm not taking a sick day.

Phil Saving them up for something big, then, are you? Some cracking pneumonia?

Carl I just know when I'm truly ill.

Phil Your nose is dripping.

Carl No, it's not.

Phil It's about to. Mate, just go home.

Carl I'm not going to cough again all day.

Phil And how are you going to do that?

Carl I'm going to will myself.

Phil Oh yeah? To victory then? Onwards to victory.

Carl You can't make me take a sickie, you know.

Phil Oh no, of course I can't.

Carl Because, in effect, you'd just be saying I'm not strong, wouldn't you?

Phil I would never want to say a thing like that.

Carl And you'd probably stick files on my desk. I know how it works.

Phil You certainly do.

Carl And these would be files with nothing at all to do with my projects.

Phil Feeling that tickle in your throat, aren't you?

Carl You have no faith in the power of the human mind.

Phil All that phlegm. Pools of it just bubbling up, ready to go.

Carl I'm a healthy person. I'm twice the employee . . .

(pause)

(long pause)

(He coughs)

Play no. 88

(Two men in suits sit at the bar in the business lounge at Heathrow)

Alan As if I wouldn't notice. As if I don't use that cologne every single day.

Gordon And it was the whole bottle?

Alan I said to her, Latvia, it's fine if you dropped the cologne. I know mistakes happen.

Gordon But you obviously don't want someone lying and stealing.

Alan Especially when they've got access to everything in the flat. And she's cleaning my other flat as well, so . . .

Gordon Her name is Latvia?

Alan That's a system I've got.

Gordon Oh.

(pause)

Oh yes, of course, of course. I see.

Alan All the syllables and all. It's easier for both of us.

Gordon It saves you mispronouncing.

Alan I just think it's disrespectful when you don't know how to say someone's name properly. So this works.

Gordon And would she be selling the stolen cologne?

Alan God knows. Or sending it back home.

Gordon You have to say something to her.

Alan I did, in a way. Do you know Suzanne, my PA?

Gordon The blonde one?

Alan No, dark hair, curly hair. After the second bottle went missing I got her to just dismiss Latvia, but politely.

Gordon You don't want to turn it into some sort of scene.

Alan You don't want to do it in a disrespectful way.

Gordon It's funny. I thought your PA had blonde hair.

Alan You might be thinking of Harry's.

Gordon Of course, of course.

Alan And now, I'm happy to say, finally there's Lithuania, which makes a nice change.

Gordon For a holiday?

Alan No, now we've got Lithuania in and she's just reliable, like clockwork, and honest.

Gordon Of course, I see. And cheap too, I imagine.

Alan You don't want to be disrespectful, do you? But that is what they're asking.

Play no. 89

(A middle-aged couple stand in a sex shop in central London)

Abi	Why? Is that strange?
Neil	It's the first time I've heard you use the word 'lapsed'.
Abi	I don't think it would feel right.
Neil	Well, choose another one, then.
Abi	No, not if you want me to be the nun.
Neil	I didn't say you had to be the nun, did I? You could be the maid.
Abi	What about the cat? With the whiskers.
Neil	I'm not doing this sort of thing with a cat. I don't like the idea behind it.
Abi	Well, I don't like the idea behind the maid.
Neil	Fine, then. What are we doing here?
Abi	We agreed this was a good suggestion. And so did Tony.
Neil	Because he's your counsellor.
Abi	He's our counsellor. It's just the maid outfit makes me think of my gran.
Neil	I don't want to think of your gran right now.
Abi	She did work in a big house, you know. In full uniform.
Neil	Not a uniform like that.
Abi	Fine, I'll be the nun then.
Neil	Oh no. Not if you're suddenly a 'lapsed' Christian.
Abi	I'm just saying there's a little belief left in me.

Neil You always used to say you weren't religious at all.

Abi It changes when you get older.

Neil You going to start going to church then?

Abi I just think there's a role for spirituality in life. I'm entitled to that.

(pause)

Neil Should we go on to the toys?

Abi You don't have to be religious to find something sacrilegious.

Neil Yes, actually. I think you do.

Abi It would be like you having to dress up as a priest.

Neil Do you want me to? This was supposed to help things.

Abi It will still help.

Neil I thought I was supposed to be the schoolboy.

Abi That's what I suggested. Yes.

Neil That doesn't work at all if you're a cat. It's not even a logical scenario for me.

Abi And it has to be about you, doesn't it?

Neil Fine. Be the cat. Be the bloody cat.

Abi I'll be the nun then. I'll be your little nun, won't I.

Play no. 90

(Two employees stand in the kitchen of an office in Reading)

Mary Well, someone should have warned you, that's what I'm saying.
Jay It's fine. I'll dash out. I'll get a sandwich.
Mary We'll pay for that. Or could you save your receipt instead?
Jay I'll keep my receipt.
Mary But we will pay you back. I'm almost sure we have money for that in the budget.
Jay It's just my sandwich was ruined. Soaked through.
Mary This happened to the last temp, too. You see, we all just know better.
Jay So, what is this liquid in the fridge?
Mary Oh, we don't know that. Do you mean its physical make-up?
Jay It was dripping. It looked quite viscous.
Mary Quite what?
Jay Quite thick.
Mary I don't think anyone's actually touched it. We just know not to put sandwiches on the shelf below.
Jay Because the container leaks?
Mary Yes, he's been bringing in that container for years.
Jay No one tells him it leaks?
Mary Oh no, no one could tell him that. He is management, after all. We just avoid him in the fridge. Keep your own sandwich to the side and you'll be all right.

Jay Does he not see the pool of liquid below?

Mary It's not our concern.

Jay And he eats whatever's in the container?

Mary Yes, every lunch hour. The office door shuts and he comes out an hour later.

Jay Is that what that terrible smell was?

Mary Which smell was that?

Jay Yesterday. On my first day.

Mary I don't remember smelling anything.

Jay It was as if an animal had died.

Mary I've been working here for a while, though. I wouldn't notice a little smell.

Jay It was in my nose the whole day and on my clothes.

Mary Temps sometimes have a problem in this environment.

Jay Will that puddle be at the bottom of the fridge tomorrow?

Mary Oh no. It gets taken care of each night.

Jay By who?

Mary By someone else. I mean, it can't be too bad. He eats it, after all.

Jay I'm going to say something to him. For all of us.

Mary Oh. We'd all prefer if it wasn't a temp who mentioned anything. He does have seniority. And there is plenty of room for your sandwich. To the side.

Play no. 91

(A woman enters the stationery room in an office in Chelmsford)

Andy Oh yeah, sure. Take any pen you want, really.

Sally Even the expensive ones?

Andy For you, yeah.

Sally I should fill my pockets.

Andy Do you know Dave who works here?

Sally Is he the one with the rash?

Andy It's more of a birthmark, like. He says I should charge people.

Sally What, for our own stationery?

Andy There should be, like, a toll.

Sally It belongs to all of us.

Andy I know, but he's like, you should get people to give you a kiss in return for a pen.

Sally A what?

Andy Not the men and all, but maybe . . . not all the women but . . .

Sally I think I just want a pen.

Andy He was totally joking and I wouldn't do it anyway.

Sally You might be let go fairly quickly.

Andy I would never do that anyway. It's just a funny thought, isn't it? Dave's funny like that.

Sally Is he? Could I get some Post-its as well?

Andy He's got all these theories. He says we've got what everyone wants.

Sally It's just stationery, though. It belongs to all of us.

Andy He says it belongs to the people but we're its guardian.

Sally You two are not exactly Mao Zedong.

Andy It's the people's Post-its. That's what he'd say. Dave studied politics and he's always saying to me we control the stationery. We could use that someday.

Sally To force people to kiss you?

Andy No, no, that was a total joke. That was just stupid.

Sally I'm going to need some staples too.

Andy But Dave says we could take over the office by controlling the means of production.

Sally You don't have the computers.

Andy Yeah, I know.

Sally Or the phones. Or anything, really.

Andy It would have to be a smaller revolution.

Sally Tiny.

Andy But still effective. You know? At least in this office. I just want to let you know, if it does start . . .

Sally Your revolution?

Andy You can take refuge here. If it gets out of hand and things really kick off. You'll have as many pens as you want.

Play no. 92

(A middle-aged man sits across the table from two younger team leaders at a marketing firm in Bristol)

Tom	You know, I could learn how to use a BlackBerry.
Nico	It's not about learning to use one.
Tom	But I could if that's what this is about.
Ryan	We really value you and your experience.
Nico	And you've had a lot of experience, Tom.
Ryan	You've been here a long time.
Nico	Some say too long, though we don't listen to that kind of talk, obviously.
Ryan	We don't agree with that.
Tom	Who said that? Did someone on the team say that?
Ryan	Exactly. Who said that? Why are these sentiments in the air? It shouldn't be listened to.
Nico	You're really one of the old school, Tom. And I think we all admire how you stick to . . . How would you put it?
Ryan	That old-school manner.
Nico	Yeah, the old-school way of doing things.
Ryan	No matter what comes along, no matter how much new technology is introduced.
Nico	Because there's no reason you absolutely have to use it.
Ryan	Though it does, you know, sometimes help the rest of us.
Tom	I've never been opposed to retraining.

Nico And we're not opposed to retraining. It's just not naturally . . . I don't know how to say it.

Ryan It's not naturally something we do.

Nico Our focus is more on training than retraining.

Tom I know the technology.

Ryan No one ever said you didn't.

Nico We haven't heard that from anyone.

Tom And I use it. Do you know how many emails I send over the course of a day?

Nico It's not about how many you send.

Tom Seventeen. Yesterday I sent seventeen.

Ryan It's more the way you send them.

Nico No one's asking you to send more emails.

Ryan But no one's asking you to walk over and ask a person if they've received the email.

Tom I like speaking to people face-to-face.

Nico Which is great, which is really old school.

Ryan I think, from what we've heard, people are just a little . . . They've moved past talking.

Nico They think it's easier to . . . I don't know how to say it.

Ryan Just express themselves through email.

Nico Your whole focus on demanding face-to-faces . . .

Ryan I just don't think it has a place here. It's great.

Nico It's old school. All that face-to-face stuff. But it's not always suitable in our office.

Tom So you're letting me go?

Nico Well, I don't really know how to say this.

Ryan It's sort of, kind of, hard to find the right words, management-wise.

Nico I think what we're trying to say is we'll email you a decision.

Play no. 93

(A man and his grown son sit by Morecambe Bay)

Reg I'll set it right, though.

Rick She's not looking for you to set it right.

Reg I'm going to. That's what your dad's going to do.

Rick It's not like she even cares any more.

Reg I'm not asking you to believe me but I'm going to set things right with your mum. I didn't run away, you know.

Rick No one's saying you ran away.

Reg I just took a breather, know what I mean?

Rick Have you even got a house up here?

Reg The room's got a cooker in it. I can show it to you.

Rick I don't want to see it.

Reg And I can almost see the water from the window. Beautiful bay, isn't it?

Rick It looks like mud.

Reg The water does come in, too, you know.

Rick Don't they get all sorts drowning out in this bay?

Reg Not everyone's out there drowning themselves.

Rick It's a bit grim, though.

Reg It's a beautiful town if you'd visited when I asked you to. Don't blame the bay. It's a good place here.

Rick I'm glad you found a good place to go to.

Reg Just for a breather. I didn't run away, you know. Now are you still playing football?

Rick No.

Reg And are you still playing in your band?

Rick No.

Reg Well, you weren't far from my thoughts, lad. I know I didn't sound my best when I called on your birthday.

Rick It wasn't my birthday, Dad.

Reg Well, I was wishing you a happy birthday.

Rick It was six months after my birthday.

Reg You were never far from my thoughts.

Rick Is that a tattoo on your hand?

Reg Oh that. Sure.

Rick Why did you get a tattoo, Dad?

(pause)

Reg Well this is just smashing, isn't it? Seeing the bay. Seeing you. I want to set things right, you know. I'm going to do that.

Play no. 94

(A man approaches a bar in central London)

Whose bag is that over by the door?

ACKNOWLEDGEMENTS

Thank you to Hugh Anderson, George and Jo Jo Rideout, Greg and Maggie Tuck, Naomi Jones and Alison McElwain, who taught me the importance of good scenes and quiet observation.

To Julie Bridgewater, Lynsey Hanley, Jamie and Jonathon O'Brien and Catalina Montoya for their donations.

To Euan Thorneycroft, Helen Garnons-Williams, Erica Jarnes, Penelope Beech, and all at Bloomsbury. To Merope Mills, Kath Viner, and Bill Mann at the *Guardian*, and, of course, Bob Granleese, who made the tiny tinier with great skill.

To Benoit Jacques, Paul Davis and Adam Simpson for the visuals.

Thank you to Scott Taylor, Marian Luxton, and Clare Taylor for the support, even from far away, and to Romola for a million tiny reasons.

A NOTE ON THE AUTHOR

Craig Taylor's non-fiction has appeared in the most prominent newspapers in three countries: the *Guardian*, the *New York Times* and the *Globe and Mail*. His fiction has appeared in the *Mississippi Review*. For the past few years he has been writing *One Million Tiny Plays About Britain* for the *Guardian*'s Weekend magazine. Three of these plays were printed on handbags and given to the winners at the Cannes Film Festival. He publishes his own photocopied magazines, including *The Review of Everything I've Ever Encountered* and *Dark Tales of Clapham*. His first book, *Return to Akenfield*, was published by Granta in 2006.

DIFF • WATFORD • LONDON • WINCHESTER • SHEFFIELD • STRATFO

EWCASTLE • EVESHAM • IPSWICH • CROYDON • LICHFIELD • NEW

ONDON • SWANSEA • GLASGOW • KING'S LYNN • BRISTOL • BIRM

HMOND • MANCHESTER • LEICESTER • LEEDS • MANCHESTER • LEW

ORTSMOUTH • WHITSTABLE • NORWICH • LANCASTER • SNOWDON

ELMSFORD • BRISTOL • YORK • MORECAMBE BAY • WATFORD • LON

BEXLEY • STANSTED • STOCKTON-ON-TEES • NEWCASTLE • EVES

DERBY • BARKING • MANCHESTER • LIVERPOOL • LONDON • SWA

ATHROW • MANCHESTER • PORTSMOUTH • CARDIFF • HENLEY-ON-TH

LEWISHAM • WATFORD • EGHAM • NORWICH • BOOTLE • HEATHROW

OWDONIA • CROYDON • CHEAM • LOUTH • BARKING • READING • C

WINCHESTER • SHEFFIELD • STRATFORD UPON AVON • ROTHERHAM

WICH • CROYDON • LICHFIELD • NEWCASTLE • NOTTINGHAM • DERBY

ING'S LYNN • BRISTOL • SUFFOLK • BIRMINGHAM • HEATHROW • MA

NCHESTER • LEICESTER • LEEDS • MANCHESTER • LEWISHAM • WATF

HITSTABLE • NORWICH • LANCASTER • SNOWDONIA • CROYDON • C

RECAMBE BAY • WATFORD • LONDON • WINCHESTER • SHEFFIELD •

TEES • NEWCASTLE • EVESHAM • IPSWICH • CROYDON • LICHFIE

ERPOOL • LONDON • SWANSEA • GLASGOW • KING'S LYNN • BRISTO

ARDIFF • HENLEY-ON-THAMES • RICHMOND • MANCHESTER • LEIC

EATHROW • GRIMSBY • PORTSMOUTH • WHITSTABLE • NORWICH

ATHROW • READING • CHELMSFORD • BRISTOL • YORK • MORECAMBE

ON • ROTHERHAM • BEXLEY • STANSTED • STOCKTON-ON-TEES • NE